Paul Curtis is a works director for a firm of cold-forging engineers. He has traveled extensively in Eastern Europe and Russia during the Cold-war years – once being arrested and interrogated by the K.G.B. in the former Soviet Union. He now lives in Surrey.

His interests are Eastern European and Russian History – political and military. He is an animal lover and supporter of Compassion in World Farming and The Donkey Sanctuary.

He is due to complete his second novel shortly.

THE
SHOCK TUBE

Paul Curtis

The Shock Tube

Vanguard Press

VANGUARD PAPERBACK

© Copyright 2004
Paul Curtis

The right of Paul Curtis to be identified as author of
this work has been asserted by him in accordance with the
Copyright, Designs and Patents Act 1988

All Rights Reserved

No reproduction, copy or transmission of this publication
may be made without written permission.
No paragraph of this publication may be reproduced,
copied or transmitted save with the written permission of the publisher,
or in accordance with the provisions
of the Copyright Act 1956 (as amended).

Any person who does any unauthorised act in relation to
this publication may be liable to criminal
prosecution and civil claims for damage.

A CIP catalogue record for this title is
available from the British Library

ISBN 1 84386 146 1

Vanguard Press is an imprint of
Pegasus Elliot MacKenzie Publishers Ltd.
www.pegasuspublishers.com

First Published in 2004

Vanguard Press
Sheraton House Castle Park
Cambridge England

Printed & Bound in Great Britain

Dedication

In memory of my dear friend Bill Cadman, killed at
Lockerby 21st December 1988

She was coming back! The disturbance of this thought caused Franz Steiner to pause with a fork halfway to his mouth. He was too excited, too agitated to eat. He returned the fork, with a slice of veal neatly folded around it, to its white china plate, and looked around surreptitiously. The refectory was busy and, it seemed to Steiner's over-excited nerves, unbearably noisy. Faces across the table were turned to each other in animated conversation. There was Hirsch, head of the mathematics department, sitting in a stiff uncomfortable looking position: tilted slightly backwards to relieve his ever-present back pain; he listened with a faint smile on his weak mouth to an aggressive tirade from an ill-humoured engineer at his side. Hirsch's plate was as untouched as Steiner's, its contents secondary in importance to debate. In contrast, next to the engineer, a white-haired, hook-nosed figure was stabbing at the last remnants of his food impatiently. This was Schellenberg, a physicist with such an outstanding brain that he was second to none in seniority, but whose title as head of physics was something of a misnomer: he had to be organised and directed by those who were supposedly his subordinates.

His purposeful demolition of his meal did not fit with the vagueness of his watery grey eyes. Schellenberg was not hungry; eating was a routine he undertook only to fulfil a promise to his wife, to be got over with as soon as possible before pushing his chair back with an expression of guilty apology, like a well brought-up child excusing himself from table to return to his toys, which in Schellenberg's case were the sub-atomic particles of his study.

After all this time, so many years, she was coming back! In spite of having overcome the initial shock of this news, Steiner had not fully accepted the reality of it: any day now he would be confronted by her physical presence. He forced himself to think of this terrifying and wondrous proposition. He was distracted by a rattling noise, and looking down saw that his hand trembled violently, agitating the fork against his plate. He frowned at this weakness and looked away from his aberrant hand, refusing to indulge it, seeing it as a temperamental child whose tantrums should be ignored. But his petulant nerves would not be subdued. A white tureen in front of him shimmered disconcertingly with refracted light as if viewed through a prism. The babble of conversation seemed suddenly unbearable. He got up hurriedly, sweating with confusion, muttered farewells to his neighbours and made his escape.

Outside he turned away from the low grey laboratory complex towards his apartment. The state of his nerves alarmed him; he would take the afternoon off and give himself time to recover. It was understandable; it was not so many years ago that he lived in constant pain from her memory – and now she was to return.

A light summer breeze cooled the sweat on his face. The worn cobblestones underfoot twisted his steps awkwardly. The sensation was comforting, reminding him of his childhood days in Brandenburg. So many of the old roads had been tarmacked over, but this place had escaped; once the road from Magdeburg to Belzig, it was now sealed-off within the scientific establishment and time had passed it by.

He jumped at the sound of an explosion and looked up into an empty sky. It was as if the sonic boom had answered the challenge of his thoughts. Fighter-jets from the nearby airfield had an unnerving habit of breaking the sound barrier overhead. The Director had complained: the shock waves interfered with some of the laboratory instruments, but the nuisance only increased, which was no surprise: the Soviet air-force was not answerable to civilians in the German Democratic Republic.

He turned into his apartment block with an apprehension he had not felt for many years. Letting himself in, he paused at the door to his spare bedroom. There had been a time when that room had been fearful to him, when he would keep the door closed, shutting away its bitter memories; until one night, his head spinning with drink, he had flung the door open with defiance to confront the ghosts that had made that place their own: a different place, changed without alteration in furniture or decoration but occupying a different space in his mind. In time, the old memories were overlain with new ones and the room became comfortable again. His fear now was that this news would work some mysterious process of reversion, and that the room would switch back to that other dreadful place, and he was relieved at the vision of comfortable tranquillity that greeted him. The freshly made bed was ready for visitors. The scene from the window was of cattle grazing in the pastures beyond the laboratories, with the dark muddled architecture of Magdeburg as a distant backdrop.

He turned away, leaving the door open, fancifully thwarting the designs of anaerobic ghosts that could multiply behind a closed door. He sat at his desk. He knew that she was coming back, but when? And where would she stay? He tried to remember exactly what had been said, but in his excitement he had forgotten all detail of the conversation.

The blank desk accused. He would be expected back at work by now; it would be discourteous not to return without explanation – but somehow at that moment even the thought of making a telephone call overwhelmed him.

He passed the afternoon without awareness – in stagnation of thought that only stirred with the fading light. Then he awoke to the memory of her return: it was around him like a choking gas. He let himself out into the evening to try and clear this inner suffocation. It was only when the street lights above him snapped on at some unseen switch that he became aware of his surroundings. He was surprised to find that he had walked through and around the main laboratory complex into an expanse of annexes on the far side – a place he had not visited for many years; a place full of memories, and unlike his spare room, the door had not been opened on them since that time – her time. But like some nocturnal animal scampering along its familiar run, he headed unerringly through the streets and alleys towards the most painful and forbidden of all places: the rooms where she had once lived. His step faltered at the end of a broad avenue lined by residential blocks on each side. His legs propelled him unbidden, his breath restricted as if his heart and lungs were squeezed by an iron grip.

The apartments were unchanged; some were in darkness, others lit from behind green orange, yellow or red curtains. The shadows and colours streamed past him in a blur. A dark space, unclosed by curtains, grew closer. His step slowed to a halt alongside a familiar street-light set on a steel girder; its light played through the window above him, projecting mysterious blocks of light and shadow into the room, illuminating the top of a picture, the spur of a wall and the corner of a cupboard. He stood looking up, half-mesmerised. It was possible to believe that time had not touched this place. The steel girder was at his shoulder; she still lived there, sitting in the darkness somewhere in the shadows of that unlit room. He turned away and continued down the street, his gaze now bowed down, pausing only to turn before that special place was out of sight. He caught his breath at the sight of the window now ablaze with light. A shadow moved; a figure paced up and down – restless just as she. He turned away, afraid of indulging this fancy any further, afraid that in the knowledge of her return his fragile state of mind could bring the past to life. At the end of the street he crossed a weed-strewn paved precinct. The spell was broken. Her street was the gateway to a past he had not visited for countless years, and now the fear of this place held him no longer. His step hurried, delivering him firmly and purposefully to his inevitable destination: a place of wonder, shut down like a ghost-town in his memory, re-animated only in dreams; but now that he was to see it again his step broke into a run and his heart pounded with excitement.

A familiar cluster of mercury lights beckoned across the

precinct. Long before being distinguishable as music, he heard the thump of bass, so deep that he felt it as a vibration in the air.

And he was stopped, his legs almost failing under him as if that distant music was a shock-wave holding him back with irresistible force. A wave of nostalgia burst inside him. His mouth opened as if to cry out. He was unprepared for the music and its power of connection to that time. He approached the heavy oak doors and stared at the iron fittings, so familiar that it seemed impossible for so many years to have passed since he had last seen them. The music bore him forwards; his hand reached for the iron ring.

Steiner had been at the laboratories for six years when she came into his life. He mused afterwards on the mechanism of fate that caused their paths to cross. In fact, statistics being his particular discipline, he even attempted to calculate the probability. Although he was soon defeated by the overwhelming variability associated with human behaviour, he amused himself with the observation that his side of the equation could easily be resolved – HIS arrival at the laboratories had been almost inevitable. From an early age he had shown an aptitude for mathematics that was matched only by his ineptitude at all other subjects. Like many mathematicians, his brilliance was more obvious to others than to himself, and his memories of schooldays were of frustration at his lack of choice rather than elation at his success. He passed effortlessly into the state university in Berlin, where he felt only sighing admiration for his colleagues who varied in every respect but one: the universal glamour of their chosen subjects over his. Mathematics seemed to him the most contemptible of all the sciences. He felt little satisfaction at the achievement of a first class degree, and little more at his effortless passage to a doctorate; it seemed too easy to be worthwhile. Only his election to the mathematics chair was a source of some pride: to be a professor at the age of thirty was unusual and a pleasant surprise. But this pride was short-lived. When, two years later, he joined the elite defence establishment at Magdeburg, he found himself amongst the greatest brains in the German Democratic Republic and his feeling of humility was double-stamped by the culture of academic snobbery that flourished under communism. Even as his career progressed and he achieved seniority, it seemed to him that the growing ranks of his juniors were to be envied: for being that vital few years younger, for their arrogant self-assurance, for their pursuit of real science as chemists, engineers or physicians, rather than a stuffy mathematician who was an appendage to science rather than a pioneer. As if to confront him with this unfavourable comparison, he acquired a representative specimen of this new breed as a neighbour.

Boris reminded Steiner of a large bear. He was broad and powerful with a slow slouching walk. His hair was long and dark, at a distance blending into a thick black pelt with the heavy coat he invariably wore. And as Steiner got to know him the likeness persisted. Boris was laconic and intense, speaking with a deep Prussian accent that was almost a growl. His eyes were close-set and so dark as to have little definition.

By nature, Boris was Steiner's opposite: brash, aggressive, opinionated and contemptuous. And yet from the first wary neighbourly greetings grew a steady acquaintance that turned into friendship. Boris' youthful assumption of superiority, which Steiner's low self-opinion would readily have granted to a stranger, came to irritate and challenge him. They clashed on almost every subject, from politics to religion, but their common battleground was science. Boris, while inferior in position, considered himself to be one of the new elite, at the forefront of the nascent computer technology, that would inevitably supersede the traditional sciences. He was impatient in discussion, convinced he was right, and when frustrated became ill-tempered to the point of being abusive. He accused Steiner, who was ten years his senior, of having the attitudes of an old man, lacking vision and refusing to accept the true position out of obstinacy. Steiner in turn was irritated by his friend's arrogance; it seemed to him that Boris, while undoubtedly intelligent, had relinquished the power of free thought, and accepted without question the fashionable position. But Steiner's irritation was tempered by amusement at his friend's lack of self-control. He found this endearing rather than offensive; behind it he glimpsed an earnest and sensitive nature, and one that was not nearly as self-assured as it appeared.

In time their discussions strayed into the personal. The first allusion to HER was so casual as to have passed unnoticed. Boris had acquired a new colleague. Her name was Hannah-Lore Sahbinger, from which her nickname derived: Sabine. She was a metallurgist, fresh from the University of Dresden. She was joining a project run by Boris' department, working on the miniaturisation of printed circuit boards – and she was attractive. Steiner had smiled at the momentary pause and fleeting thoughtful expression that had followed this observation. From that first mention she featured ever more prominently in Boris's conversation. Steiner found this tedious at first. He had not even met the girl and yet she came to usurp their scientific/philosophical discussions. It came as no surprise to him, a week later, to learn from Boris that the two were a couple, although he was amazed at the speed of their courtship. And in time his attention was drawn to the unseen drama that he guessed the course of, by the change in his friend's mood; Boris' natural gloom gave way to a vivacity and elation that was almost skittish.

This both touched and amused Steiner. But he tactfully refrained from pronouncing his diagnosis: Boris was in love.

Boris evidently repeated the many arguments between him and Steiner to Sabine. She became an invisible adjudicator between them. Boris relayed her verdicts: "Sabine says to tell you that you're a reactionary and that she has a friend in the STASI who is very interested in your views and wishes to discuss them with you." And on another occasion: "Sabine is shocked by your cynicism – seriously shocked – I mean it. I told her what you said, and she was really angry. I've not seen her like that before. She says she will not speak to you." And Boris and Steiner had laughed at the idea of Sabine's deep sulk against Steiner whom she had never met.

After some weeks, Boris's mood began to change again. He became more thoughtful and withdrawn. Steiner was concerned. He had formed some strong impressions of this girl, even though they were second-hand. She was wild, spirited, and wilful. He could imagine the Boris of the past few weeks – light-hearted, careless and boisterous – to be attractive to her, but Boris was returning to his old self. In a fanciful moment, Steiner was reminded of a fairy-tale his grandmother had told him as a child: of a man who turned at night into a bear. And Boris was more morose, intense and bear-like than ever. At the same time, the light-hearted banter that Boris had become the messenger of, between Steiner and Sabine, changed its substance, becoming more pointed and challenging. While Sabine took Steiner's side in many arguments, she took what seemed to Steiner exaggerated affront at some of his remarks that Boris had repeated to her. One day her distant irritation reached a crescendo. Boris and Steiner had been discussing an argument between two women in their department. Boris was bewildered by the argument. The two women had been close friends and had fallen out over something apparently trivial. Steiner had suggested that the real reason underlay the argument, expanding this to claim that most women communicated with each other at a subliminal level, that the language of their eyes and movements was the real conversation, with little connection to their spoken words. Boris had repeated this to Sabine and had been surprised by her anger. She paced up and down in sullen silence, finally bursting into a tirade against Steiner. Boris shook his head with bemusement as he related this. "She says you don't understand women, which she says she would forgive were it not for your belief to the contrary."

Steiner laughed. "I give way to her superior knowledge of course. What's her explanation?"

"Don't know. She doesn't say. It's strange: she's so angry with you and yet it's just the sort of thing she would have said herself."

"There you are, you see — the very reason: we are in competition — my intuition against hers."

It was shortly after this conversation that Steiner met Sabine. He wondered afterwards whether her irritation at his repeated views had inspired the confrontation. And yet when she turned up unexpectedly one evening with Boris, she greeted him as a stranger, making the messages which had passed between them seem like a fantastic invention. She met his smile of curiosity with a fleeting uninterested glance. His first impression was of her height. He could see that she was beautiful, with a graceful figure and upright carriage, and with the hauteur that he guessed went with awareness of her looks. This amused him; she was of a type not attractive to him. Her skin was spectacularly pallid against the darkness of her hair and eyes. It had an almost unhealthy translucence as if she had been incarcerated as a child in a darkened room. A splash of colour in her cheeks added to the contrast of her face. Steiner found himself musing on whether in later life this would give way to broken capillaries. His attention was soon drawn to Boris, who was acting most strangely. He ignored Sabine by looking pointedly away from her, so much so that he achieved a comic effect by overhanging the end of the sofa, like a little boy in a sulk at his mother. He got up to help himself to a drink. His self-consciousness expressed itself as an awkward slouching bear-like gait. He sank heavily back onto the sofa with a brooding sullen expression that found words in a sudden attack on Steiner.

"So then — thought any more of our discussion? I'm sure I'm wasting my breath but one has to hope. One day you'll wake up — you and Hirsch and all the other old fossils in your department. It needs a good earthquake in there just to drown the sound of snoring."

Steiner was taken aback. He was used to Boris's ill-temper in argument but this was so sudden and inappropriate as to be extraordinary, and he studied his friend to see if this were a rare display of humour, while protesting mildly:

"Dear me – you sound like you've just wiped out the Kulaks and want to start on mathematicians!"

Boris leant forward with an intense frown; he didn't like being mocked. "You make a joke of it, but in truth you are holding us back. You're standing in our way – in the way of progress – with a frown of discouragement a shake of your head or a patronising smile." Boris tore at his hair in a gesture of frustration that Steiner again found peculiar for being untypical of his friend. "Our science, computer science, is the way forward and you can't or you won't embrace it. Deep in your heart you know it will overtake you and you'll be left behind – guardians of the museum that your calculations and your formulae have become."

Steiner lost the thread of this rant. He now understood that Boris was showing off by presenting himself as impetuous and passionate and demonstrating his contemptuous familiarity with his senior. He found himself studying Boris' expression and saw that his friend would not meet his eyes. This confirmed his theory: Boris had a simple honest nature and the falseness of this debate made it impossible for him to meet Steiner's gaze.

Steiner was embarrassed for his friend as he watched his performance, grimacing and flourishing with his hands. This was Boris as he had never seen him before; these were the pathetic steps of a dancing bear, tormented from his slouching gait into a grotesque pirouette. Steiner found his attention drawn to the girl sitting silently and looking casually around the room apparently bored by the conversation; and suddenly he divined her role: she was the bear-trainer, half the creature's weight and yet driving the poor lumbering beast with a sting from her whip up onto his back legs.

Steiner watched her from the periphery of his vision and

was afraid for his friend. There was something dreadful about the dynamics of this relationship: Boris so in love, all his gravity abandoned in an attempt to impress – and she.... What satisfaction did she derive from her supreme control over him? Was the bear-trainer in truth a bear-baiter – and his humiliation her twisted reward? Or was this her part in a convoluted plot that must be enacted in precise detail by both players in order to share in a final act of love – just as the complicated mating ritual of some exotic species of bird?

This was the first of many visits. Sabine unbent a little towards Steiner. Instead of greeting him as a stranger, a momentary lapse in the hauteur of her expression acknowledged that she had met him before. On one visit she got up to walk around the room, apparently interested in the few but precious belongings that Steiner allowed as decoration. She picked up an ancient ship's clock that he had inherited from his Grandfather. She handled it carefully and examined it minutely; it appeared to please and intrigue her. Steiner was amused by the contradiction of her distant greeting to him and this rather impolite scrutiny of his possessions. She moved on to a square brass plate with a bulbous distortion in its centre, picked it up and interrupted Boris's flow of animated conversation to ask:

"This has come out of a shock-tube?"

Steiner took the plate from her. "Yes. It failed to burst. You can see where it's been weakened." He traced with his finger across an 'H' pattern of grooves cut across the underside of the distorted bulb. "You're a metallurgist – I'd be interested to know why that happened. The tube got up to pressure – I can't remember the exact figures, but it was something like fifty per cent in excess of the burst-pressure."

She stared directly and searchingly into his eyes. He found this disconcerting. Her attention returned to the plate. She appeared to consider.

"There are several possibilities: tensile strength, internal structure, impurities, but I wouldn't expect such a wide variation in burst pressure; no, I think it is probably to do *with composition. Someone in procurement has tried to make a saving by using a cheaper alloy, I expect."*

She handed him the plate and he took it from her with a smile. "I see – thank you." She stared at him with the same curious expression in her eyes, and he looked away. His shyness came from his thoughts: she would laugh at him or ridicule him if she knew them: this plate was precious to him for its resilience; it had been subjected to a pressure of nearly twenty tonnes per square centimetre, and survived against the odds. It was a special plate and an inspiration to him. Sabine reached out to touch the grooves of the plate. She caressed them absent-mindedly, as if forgetting for a moment where she was; and when she spoke, Steiner did not realise at first that she addressed him.

"It withstood the blast. They couldn't break it. That's what makes it special to you."

Steiner looked at her in surprise. Across the room, he was troubled to see that Boris stared at him moodily. Steiner understood. Her eyes were turned once more towards him with an interest and animation that he had not seen directed towards Boris. She smiled.

"I'm like that – just a few things with no value that anyone would understand." Her long slender fingers drew away from the plate. She smiled distantly as if to herself and at that moment a chiming tune as if from a musical-box invaded the silence. Steiner traced the sound to a movement of her hand in her pocket. She withdrew an open silver locket and raised it to Steiner. "See?"

He saw that the locket was intricately crafted and so tiny and delicate that it was hard to believe that it concealed any mechanism. She offered it up so that he could see facing him a miniature portrait in the open lid. He studied it with interest. At first glance it was the face of an old woman with the rigid poise and expression belonging to an age long past. But as he looked closer he saw that the woman's age was exaggerated by the brown coloration of the early days of bromide photography and the severity of her swept-back hair and high collar of a fashion that dated back to the Kaisers. She was perhaps in early middle-age, and the longer he looked at her the more fascinating became the face, staring back at him with character, defiance and a beauty undiminished by the sternness of her expression.

He looked up to see a curious expression on Sabine's face: a half-smile that was almost mocking. But Boris' reaction was more curious. He sat forward staring with intensity. Steiner mused. Which mood of the bear was this? An alert bear, at the entrance to his lair, checking the air with the knowledge of intruders, ready to defend himself?

Sabine snapped the locket shut. Her voice was distant as if disconnected to her words. "My great grand-mother. A proud and beautiful woman, and very well-connected – not something to be proud of perhaps; she would not have been a disciple of Rosa Luxembourg I'm afraid." Steiner hid a smile. Her smirk of approval denied the orthodoxy of her words.

In the following days, Steiner became progressively more puzzled and concerned about the affair. His visitors sat so far away from each other on the sofa that it was almost a statement. She reminded Steiner of girls he had known at university, willing to be his friend but pre-empting anything more physical by keeping an exaggerated distance from him. And Steiner recognised his friend's behaviour: Boris' every sense was alert to her, every word laden with the assumption that she listened. He tried every turn. Sometimes, as if stung by the rebuff of her evident lack of interest, he would turn his back on her and engage Steiner in exclusive conversation. But then, in a feigned attempt at quixotry, he would turn suddenly to her, including her, bathing her in the light of his renewed interest, and, carried away by his own charm, he would bend towards her, drawn helplessly like a phototropic plant to the light. She could have summoned him with the slightest encouragement, the play of a smile on her lips, and he would have fawned upon her. And occasionally she would feed this ravenous bear a morsel so small that it seemed to Steiner a torment rather than sustenance. She would touch his arm or smile into his eyes with animation, and that great lumbering beast would rock on his feet, overwhelmed with gratitude, stumbling over his words, pathetically unmanned.

One day, Sabine called on Steiner without Boris. She had lost a bracelet and wondered if she had dropped it on her last visit. They searched and sure enough it had slipped down the back of the sofa. Steiner hid his scepticism and wondered at the purpose of this visit. Her eyes were averted from his. It occurred to him that she was not naturally deceitful. She appeared artificially relieved at recovering the bracelet. She spoke of how precious it was to her. He played along, interested to know where this was leading. He offered her a drink and she accepted. Observing her, he admitted to himself that there was a glamour about her that had not impressed him before. She wore a white blouse tucked into black slacks, which accentuated her wide hips. Her body was slightly out of proportion to her height: her legs too short and her back too long, giving her a shape that did not conform to a classical ideal but was nonetheless becoming. The high colour in her cheeks, which he had at first faulted, he now observed contrasted with the sheen of her short dark hair. But it was her eyes, turned unexpectedly towards him, that disconcerted him. She studied him for a long moment as if aware of his appraisal and challenging him. Her expression was intent, questioning and sexual. His thoughts tumbled out disjointedly – wondering if she was aware of the blatancy of that long stare, wondering if she was truly suddenly curious about him – but above all, confused as to the nature of the girl. This moment he recognised afterwards as a turning point, marking a new curiosity and interest in her.

Shortly after this incident, Boris came late one night to Steiner's apartment and opened his heart. Steiner was both surprised and embarrassed. Boris had always treated his senior with condescension, and Steiner was humbled by his friend's abandonment of pride to suffer this intimacy. The explanation was soon revealed. Boris had fallen in love with Sabine and was helplessly bewildered by her behaviour towards him. He spoke as Steiner had never heard before: directly from the heart; and Steiner, touched by this honesty and earnestness, listened with sympathy.

"I don't know what she wants. She will spend an evening with me. She looks into my eyes – her eyes, they melt my soul. She drinks with me, laughs with me. I should explain, sometimes she gets quite drunk, she leans against me, clasps my arm with her hand. I can't explain – you would have to see how it is. I know everything is right, that we will caress and be lovers. Evening turns to night. We sit with the windows open enjoying the night. She doesn't want to go home. It's late and I tell her I must go to bed, and she follows me clasping my hand. She likes to hold my hand – you've not seen that, she won't in front of others – but it's strange. It's like a child holding its mother's hand rather than a lover's. We go to bed; I swear it's because she doesn't want to be alone. She will sleep against me, her hand still in mine. We are lovers in all but the act. And then in the morning..." Boris ran his hand through his hair. Steiner observed to himself that this was an agitated bear; dangerous emotion lurked under the dark silky fur. "And then, in the morning, she is cold, frigid, scared – resentful even, as if regretting the night before." Boris laughed harshly. "Regretting what? It is seldom enough, twice to be precise, and both times she was so drunk I'm not even sure she knew what she was doing – until the morning – then her coldness was like ice." Boris paused to light a cigarette. "I've never been like this – not with anyone." He looked up suddenly, his face red with shame. "I'm sorry, going on like this. I can't talk to anyone else, they wouldn't understand."

Steiner touched his friend briefly on the hand, not trusting himself to speak, overwhelmed by a sudden affection for his friend stripped of all affectation, speaking from the heart – a trembling naked bear.

Boris looked away awkwardly. "If only I knew how she felt. Yesterday, we were walking back from the labs. I took her hand, I couldn't help myself. She wouldn't take it. She looked afraid! I don't think of me but of what people might think. She is particularly cold in any place where we might be seen. She walks apart from me. She hates the thought of being talked about, particularly to you, strangely enough. Several times she has made me promise not to discuss her with you. And now..." He laughed again, almost hysterically. *"I've told you everything – you of all people."*

Steiner mused as to why Sabine should have this particular concern. Boris answered the question in his thoughts: "I think she looks up to you – to your position. She's intensely aware of position."

Steiner detected a slight resentment and understood what had not been clear to him before: he had taken Boris's confrontational debating to be an attempt to impress Sabine; he had not understood that it was an attempt to diminish him before her eyes.

The dance hall was much as Steiner remembered it, except for the disc jockey's alcove, which had been raised up on stilts to oversee the throng of dancers. A youth jabbered conversationally into a microphone that appeared to be glued to his lips, while he searched frantically through a box of records. His patter borrowed heavily from the American forces radio stations that pumped out VHF radio across the GDR to an avid communist audience. This was a boldness that would not have been attempted in the past. Steiner was amused by the contrast of the disc jockey's pretensions, to the area beneath him where drinks were served from trestle tables.

He imagined that people watched him with curiosity, and was grateful to retire to the fringe of the dance-floor, dimly lit by orange light. The music pounded in his ears. It came as a surprise to him to find that his body was swaying to the rhythm. His limbs moved naturally, gaining in confidence. He was fifty-eight years old and he was dancing!

The visits from Boris continued, increasing in frequency and desperation. His composure disintegrated in the face of his increasing passion, and with it grew the carelessness of Sabine's treatment of him. He was pitifully unaware of this in his confusion. In Steiner's fancy an image formed of the bear in its pit, submitting to the cruelty of its mistress. And this suspicion of the girl's nature made Steiner particularly ashamed of his part in the affair that followed.

The dance hall at weekends was packed with a clientele that bordered on the bizarre. By a contradiction typical under communism, the decadent western music that the authorities took such pains to deny to the proletariat was a treasured privilege to the elite, and a match for any played in the discos of West Berlin. Understandably, this music was a rallying point for the youth of the complex. But it was a strange current that drew another unlikely group of enthusiasts: the most senior scientists in the establishment, moved by the peculiarity of their brilliant brains to be completely ignorant of what was fashionable or appropriate, letting their hair down in rebellion against the stuffiness of academic life. Moving with the frigid lack of rhythm which only scientists can accomplish, they danced with surreal comedy amongst the abandoned youths who served under them during the day, but who lectured them on the dance-floor. To add a final comic touch, a few ever-present STASI agents stood languidly watchful, their stiff immobility a datum point of the dance.

Steiner did not enjoy the detachment of his robotic colleagues. He was young enough to aspire to the wild abandonment of the more youthful dancers. He stood on the fringe of the dance-floor, tormented by self-consciousness until an excess of vodka loosened his inhibitions sufficiently to dive into the heaving throng, inspired by their wild movements to half-believe that his erratic dance merged with theirs.

And then one night she was there. Both were aware of each other's presence, although no sign of recognition passed between them. She was on her own. She danced well, her movements lithe and rhythmical. She appeared unaware of those around her, and yet as Steiner watched, he imagined that she manipulated them. The young men danced with an awareness of her presence, their pace increased, and it seemed that by some subliminal sense the women felt threatened and were wary of her. Her dancing increased in frenzy as if fed by this knowledge and nurtured by the mixture of admiration and hostility that surrounded her.

The music quickened its pulse and increased in volume. Some of the dancers retired to the sides of the floor. The lights flickered, creating an illusion of the dancers writhing slowly in negative. Inexorably, Sabine and Steiner were drawn together by the moving pattern until they were dancing opposite each other, together and apart.

It seemed to Steiner that she danced for him alone. He revised his opinion of her proportions; her body twisted sensuously in perfect time; it was as if the motion of her long back and swelling hips were an adaptation for the dance. His confidence disintegrated. His movements lost timing and he slowed awkwardly, feeling clumsy and uncoordinated. In the pulsing light he saw her smile, at first he thought in encouragement, but then, lit for a moment in a burst of white light, he saw her eyes glitter above the twist of her mouth with a peculiar expression of triumph. And suddenly he was in awe of her. In his imagination she grew in height. A question was settled in his mind: whatever motive she had for her treatment of Boris was with knowledge of its effect.

There was a mocking invitation in her smile; to take a step forward would be to enter into her dance, her smile and her embrace. He shrank back before the image he had created of a towering shadow behind her; but, as the weaving of a snake's head hypnotises its prey, her writhing dance entranced him. He was in her lair, in her power, commanded to perform. His hesitant movements gained in confidence, drawn into the rhythm of her dance. The music pounded in his ears, bearing him up into it. He surrendered himself, aware that he was to cross some deadly threshold from which there would be no return. In his imagination, the looming, mocking shadow shrank. The concentration of her expression was turned away, and he was relieved, safe but deflated.

Sabine came to visit regularly. She became comfortable in his presence, seldom sitting for long, sometimes studying his possessions with the open curiosity that amused him, and opening the musical locket with a regularity that he took to be a mild obsession.

They talked about science and religion, and strayed into areas of politics that were dangerous for people who knew each other so little. But the one matter never discussed was the subject of Steiner's shame and intrigue: how, at the end of each week, they danced together, sometimes smiling into each other's eyes, sometimes avoiding each other's gaze, but with never a word spoken between them. Steiner could have believed that she had a twin sister who brushed her body against his or stood still in the shadows at the side of the floor, oblivious to the music, watching him silently and intently. And when one week she did not come to his apartment, he guessed that she had decided to stop seeing him, and was unsurprised when at the end of the week she was not at the dance hall. But his sense of disappointment was extreme, making him aware of how much he had hoped she would be there, and how absurdly important this peculiar liaison had become to him. The music that night seemed unusually loud – a pulsing anthem driving the dancers into a sullen frenzy.

And then she was there, emerging from the crowd as if borne up by them – the ambassador of their dance. Her mocking smile held the knowledge of his desolation, multiplying her power. The shadow of his imagination towered over her, menacing and laughing down at him. Her body was so close that he could feel the heat that seemed to come from her hips. He was intensely aware of every deft gentle caress of her body against his. He expected that at any moment, warned by her teasing smile, she would draw away from him. But the pressure of her body increased. Her smile commanded. They kissed. She pressed herself against him. He was aware of the impropriety of their embrace amongst the dancers around them, but was careless of the world outside her embrace, as an infant child in its mother's arms. It was she that broke away and led him across the dance floor. Outside, the intimacy of her hand in his seemed suddenly shocking now that they were away from that special place where her presence existed only in fantasy.

They made love in a wooded park. Steiner felt abstracted from the physical act, his mind unable to keep pace with the speed of events, left behind, walking while his body ran, falling back, calling out, protesting about Boris, about loyalty and betrayal. And when the act of lovemaking recaptured his attention, he was aware of an almost humorous surrealism: her passion seemed remote from him; she moaned, heaved, climaxed, as if being pleasured in her dreams by some phantom lover. And when it was over, she reached for her clothes as if she was only at that moment aware of his presence and was suddenly shy of her nakedness.

Steiner finished his drink and left the dance hall. Passing the park, he averted his eyes from that place, but curiosity overcame him. The park was apparently unchanged and yet the undergrowth was thicker and the shadows darker. It was a different place, changed by time. He was relieved to escape from it back into the familiar streets.

Back in his rooms, he poured a large glass of vodka. Today had taken a toll on his nerves. His hand shook. How would he work tomorrow? How would he sleep? The spirits steadied his hand. It was as if he had awoken today from a long sleep, the turmoil of reality forgotten in his dreams. She was coming back! His hand shook again as he refilled his glass. Was this due to excitement or fear of that dreadful unrest to which he had awoken? The room rearranged itself in his mind to how it had been.

Steiner was seated. She paced in front of him.

"It's over with Boris. It should never have been. He was just a friend."

"But you slept with him." He was disconcerted by her long pause. She was thinking about what to say. It made him doubt her reply.

"It was never Boris. It's true I slept with him. I liked him and I felt sorry for him. He wanted me so much. It was something I could give him that cost me nothing." She smiled indulgently. *"Do you understand that? It wasn't unpleasant. He..."* She paused in thought. The falseness he had imagined was swept away so that he judged she was about to speak sincerely. *"He fell in love with me. I was unprepared for that."* Did he imagine a glitter of satisfaction in her eyes? Her concentration returned to him, but her eyes would not meet his. She paced the room uneasily, opened the locket, listening for a long moment to the chiming tune before speaking.

"What happened between us... I have doubts about us, about our circumstances; I don't know if it will work." Her anxieties poured out, unformed, half-incoherent, touching on all manner of problems: the imbalance in their positions, difficulties with her colleagues and seniors, her need for independence. Steiner was bemused. The one trouble in his mind – their betrayal of Boris – seemed of no concern to her, displaced by her agitation about matters which were absurdly premature to him. And he was struck as she talked on by her lack of engagement with him, just as when they had made love; these were her private thoughts expressed aloud, requiring no reply from him. As if challenged by this unspoken criticism, her eyes held his and he softened: there was something touching in her agitation and seriousness – a glimpse into a vulnerable side of her nature that he had not seen before – an opposite to the triumphal queen of the dance.

He attempted to reassure her, telling her that the single act of lovemaking was not a commitment on either side. She seemed irrationally relieved as if his reaction was unexpected *to her, and when he raised the subject of Boris, she appeared surprised and undertook with a disconcerting casualness to deal with the matter.*

Evidently she lost no time in doing so. A loud knock on the door that same evening announced Boris. He almost fell into the room, staggering drunk. Steiner was alarmed by the wild appearance of his friend. This was an aroused bear, drawn up to his full height, beating his chest with a dangerous light in his dark eyes. But Boris' bitter humour was not turned against his friend. He helped himself to a large vodka and stood breathing heavily, appearing to see Steiner for the first time.

"She wants to be friends." He spat the words.

Steiner bent his head. "I'm sorry."

Boris looked at him with a sentimentality Steiner had not seen before. "I'm not angry with you. If it had to be anyone, I'm glad it's you. You are my friend. It will be painful. I could not bear to see her again, you understand, but I want us to remain friends." He looked at Steiner humbly. "That is if you will."

Steiner was ashamed. His friend, whom he had always found arrogant and contemptuous, was revealed, and Steiner understood that these traits had been mere designs, a defence against Steiner that he had himself not understood.

Boris drank again. "Friends... That's what made me mad. I am not so proud of myself, but I couldn't help it. 'I don't give a shit about you,' is what she meant. She said it, not to be gentle, but because it was the easiest thing for her to say. When I lost my temper she was afraid, like a cornered rat, searching for soothing words to calm me down – and when that didn't work – she seduced me." He laughed bitterly. "That worked. I couldn't do it. My body wanted her. I was stiff with passion for her – that mechanism knows no subtlety – but my heart was numbed, outraged, horrified – for her. How little she cares for herself to use that so readily – picked up like a blunt instrument to defend against an attack.

And when I was weakened and quiet with disgust – for myself as much as her, at my arousal like an animal – she patronised me, like a mother offering her breast to calm a screeching brat. What sort of a woman is she? In my foolish passion I've managed to avoid that question so adroitly – but think of it and be careful. I don't say this to poison you. I know – I've known for a long time – she has some feeling for you far greater than ever she had for me, even though it hurts to say it. But I deceive myself no longer. This way I keep my sanity and my pride - and how close I came to losing them. Some shrill persuasive voice tells me that this is all a hurtful quarrel and you an invention to make me jealous – her true intention to sleep with me and mend the hurt – and by denying her I have ended it – I, you understand." Boris swallowed his drink.

His anger turned suddenly to self-pity. His eyes turned pathetically to Steiner and filled with tears. He fled from the room, banging so hard against the doorframe that the room shuddered. Steiner looked after him, afflicted with guilt and misery. This was a wounded bear, shot through the heart, subdued by emotions that had never before troubled the limited soul of a beast.

Steiner turned away, troubled. He walked reverently across the room, but the vision of this place as it had been, persisted. He stopped almost in the centre of the floor in empty space.

The lower half of her face was lit by a shaft of sunlight, highlighting her mouth and the lines of her cheeks, adding to the solemnity of her eyes in shadow, which were unsmiling. She spoke as if making an announcement.

"I don't want to mislead you. I don't know what will happen between us. I don't want to rush into anything. If you're willing to accept me as I am, with no commitment – no ties – I have to be free – and of course..." She looked at him directly for the first time; there was no doubting her sincerity. "The same applies to you."

Steiner nodded, more in acknowledgement than agreement, for again his mind was following behind. But she appeared satisfied and relieved, as before, and the conversation was ended.

She returned that night, her mood changed, needing him, holding him to her after they had made love. It was only the next day he realised that she had moved in.

His unease deepened. He understood that her protestations of needing freedom were for her own persuasion, that the pressure she felt the need to resist was not from him. His own fears were for the unnatural pace of events. He questioned how he felt about her. The image he had created in the dance hall, of the shadow towering over her, reconstructed itself. It seemed foolish to think of being in love. And there was something wrong about sex with her: it seemed to be at the call of some whim beyond her control; it was unnaturally urgent and frenetic, and left him unsure of his own part in it.

The first clue to his emotions came some nights later. She went out dancing. He wondered at this. He had assumed that her dancing had been for him; that now they were together she would have no need for it. He was aware of the arrogance of this thought but could not help musing on what she would be doing. Would her dance be as sexual? Would there be some other man she would dance close to, her hips writhing as they had for him? He had gone to bed late with these thoughts troubling him and slept uneasily. He was awoken in the early hours by the sound of a door opening. He was instantly awake and listened intently. Were there two pairs of footsteps into the other bedroom? She had taken the spare room as hers even though up until now she had shared his bed. His ears strained into the silence for a long time, and then, so softly that he wondered if he imagined it, he heard the sound of whispered voices. He felt suddenly cold, dreading the sound, and dreading the silence if it were to stop. He couldn't stand this anticipation. Getting up, he dressed silently, tiptoed to the door and closed it behind him, fearful that she should hear him. His chill turned instantly to a hot sweat at the thought of discovery.

Out into the night, he headed across the complex. There was a bar close to the laboratories, open through the night for the shift workers. He had been there before when he couldn't sleep. In his anguish, he dreaded the sound of footsteps – night-workers, lovers, police. It seemed that any casual observer must perceive the reason for his shame and demand some explanation.

The bar was full of power workers – a section of cabling into the complex was being replaced. He was grateful for their presence. He felt invisible amongst them, reassured by their muscular frames. He sat with a bottle of vodka at a corner table. He couldn't go back. His mind conjured images of Sabine with another man. He saw her naked, bowed forwards against the man's chest, her slender fingers feeling his arms that were strong and muscular, just as the power workers around him. He loved her. How unhealthy to discover this through jealousy. The vodka eased his pain. He knew he could not go back until the darkness was over. He concealed the bottle under his coat and slunk out of the bar. He wanted to be alone.

He took a turn that led towards a pedestrian avenue; he knew it was a dead-end and hoped it would be deserted. He passed a derelict church. It stood in its own pool of darkness that seemed blacker than the shadows surrounding it. He hurried past the once magnificent but now boarded-up stained-glass windows; there was something sinister about the place at night. The avenue was lit with a row of mercury lights at little more than head height due to the proximity of the northern runway of the nearby military airfield. The road ended in a pile of earthworks around an electrical switching-station. A pit exposed underground cables. Steiner squatted by the edge of the pit, for some inexplicable reason finding comfort in this place. The cables were massive – the main lines that the power workers were replacing. He sipped at the vodka, making it last until the first pale light of dawn. Now he could return. He finished the bottle in one swig. The spirit went straight to his head. He began the walk back, unsteady on his feet.

He paused at her door, straining for the sound of breathing, but all was silent. He turned to his room. She was in his bed, asleep. He slipped into bed alongside her. She murmured in her sleep but did not awaken. He slept fitfully. His dreams fed on his doubts and he witnessed her betrayal in terrible detail. When he awoke, his relief was so great to find her beside him that he was completely cowed. Her arms stretched towards him but he buried his head in her thighs in an act of submission. She was aroused to a passion he had not known before. He confessed to his doubts in the night and she held his head to her, comforting him. There had been no second pair of footsteps; the whispered conversation was her talking to herself. She admitted apologetically that this was a quirk that persisted from childhood, particularly at night.

Steiner learnt that this was true. Later in the week, he came home from working late, let himself in quietly, thinking that she might have gone to bed. He paused at the door to his room, hearing a voice. He froze in surprise. It was Sabine's voice, whispering as if contemplatively: "So clever, so beautiful. The men can't help themselves from eyeing you up and down. I'm jealous of course. You know how to keep a man, certainly. Oh, certainly – that is for certain. Of all things, that is a certainty." She laughed out aloud. "But I'll not tell you everything just yet. You've always been the interesting one, so interesting, so fascinating – and me such an open book. But then I have just one or two tiny secrets even from you – and I know you'd like to know. You'll not ask, I suppose. You would never do that. To betray that interest would be just a little demeaning wouldn't it, my sweet? It would just reduce you that tiny fraction. Be a reducing agent – as opposed to an oxidising agent – the reactant that donates the electron and becomes oxidised when another substance is reduced – let me see now, Lithium, that's a good one. Sodium hydrosulphite, that's another – and of course, this one here that you would not like to be added to the list."

Steiner guessed that this monologue could go on and on, and, ashamed of his eavesdropping, chose this moment to open the door. She had moved a chair into the centre of the room and sat there, fingering her locket, her head lowered as if in conversation with it. She started at his presence. Her eyes, wide and hunted, met his.

He knew he could not sleep; he was afraid even to try, in case the flow of memories, now started, should overwhelm him. He was summoned by the thought of that same place where he had sought sanctuary in the night. He slipped out into the street. The night was warm and yet he shivered. He turned away from the familiar streets towards the derelict church and then into the long avenue that, like the dance hall, he had not revisited since that time. The peculiar effect of the ribbon of head-high lights before him, pulled at his memory. All the time passed since he had walked along this avenue was cast aside as if it had never existed. His solitary footsteps merged with a soft echo from the past, until they were one.

His doubts returned. He accepted that he had been mistaken about hearing two pairs of footsteps on her return from the dance – and thinking about it afterwards, he realised what an absurd fancy this had been: if she were to be unfaithful to him, she would hardly bring a lover back to his apartment. But he remembered her reaction to his confession of his suspicions and suspected a connection to her passionate arousal that had followed. Her indulgence in his foolishness had been unwholesome, as if she had enjoyed it. There had been a hint of triumph in her smile. Perhaps even she had constructed his fears: her whispered conversation had been loud enough to hear from the adjoining room and yet when he had surprised her talking to herself earlier that week, he had had to strain his ears to hear her at an open door. Did she have a need to exercise power over him or was she laughing at him, making a fool of him – as careless of him as she had been of Boris? He struggled against these suspicions, recognising them as unhealthy and destructive; after all, he knew so little about her; it was only to be expected that there would be misunderstandings. He must learn to trust her. This thought allowed him at last to turn from this obsessive internal dialogue, but he was shocked by the sheer force of the storm of emotions that had been aroused by his doubts. He knew now that he was falling in love as never before. And when she went again to the dance hall, all his reassurance dissolved. His pride would not allow him to question her, but the unease was aroused in him again. Why did she need to persist with her dancing when she had him? Was her dance changed from outrageous sexual provocation into another that was modest and demure? Was she now oblivious to the presence of the men around her? These questions burned into him. There were nights when he could not sleep but could not bear the shame of lying awake in bed half the night waiting for the sound of her step on the stair. He would drink and then pace the streets, fearful that she would return and find him gone, but even more fearful to spend the night away with friends, as if without his vigilance she could slip into some act of betrayal. Each time became more unbearable. His night walks led inexorably to the dance hall – standing outside listening to the heavy thud of dance music. Eventually the pressure overcame him. One night he dressed himself in dark unfamiliar clothes and entered the dance, the pound of his heart beating in his ears in time to the music. He kept his head turned away until he was safely in the shadows at the far end from the dance floor. A glass of vodka fortified him against the fear of discovery. So he witnessed her dance; her abandonment to the music, surrounded by men summoned to her: the satellites of her dance, subjugated to her, bending towards her like flowers to the sun, hopeful that her lithe provocative rhythm would reward them with a touch of her body against them – in the same ecstasy of anticipation as he had been.

He felt sick and swallowed a mouthful of vodka to

bolster himself. His stare was unable to leave her. He calculated the distance between her and the men around her, dreading any touch, for he knew what would surely follow. In spite of his torment, it seemed that her pre-occupation did not favour any particular dancer. She weaved amongst them, lost in the music.

The pulse quickened and hardened, taken over by a harsh dissonant rhythm of bass strings. A singer's voice – feminine, powerful, melodic and haunting – infused the pounding rhythm. Sabine's mouth, frozen half-open by stroboscopic light, turned to him in song, her taunting smile directed into his eyes, illuminating the dark recess of his concealment.

He slipped away, pacing the night, testing all the possibilities in a hopeless torrent of obsessive thought. Her dance was as overt and sexual as ever. She would turn to a dancer in the heat of the moment and take him outside, just as she had him. But, his heart pleaded, why should she suddenly lose her love of music – this particular music which was hers – and dancing, just because of him? Wouldn't that be absurd? Then came another torment, making him hot with shame at the vision of her face turned in recognition towards him. Surely that could not have been his imagination? But then too, it seemed impossible that she could have sought him out in the darkness.

She returned home in the early hours. His overworked mind had eventually been pacified by vodka and he slept. She slipped into bed beside him and the warmth of her body against him lightened his dreams. He awoke with her arms around him. Her eyes contemplated him. She smiled at him as he awoke and held him to her, but his waking impression of her contemplation lingered. She gently rebuffed his attempts at lovemaking. Lying with her was a torment. The shameful suspicion came to him that she knew this. He searched her face for any sign of an answer to the question that troubled him. Had she seen him at the dance?

By some illusion the lights stretched before him appeared as a tunnel of shimmering blue. As he walked through, the light closed around him in a fine mist. He felt unsteady on his feet and had to stop, shaking his head to try and dispel the image before him, but the lights streamed and twirled. He closed his eyes, irritated by this sensation. He must have drunk too much vodka. He started off again at a brisk pace. The moving tunnel retreated to an aura around each light

He was in the habit of holding a dinner party every month for his two best friends and their wives: Schellenberg – head of physics, and Hirsch – head of mathematics. Boris was inspired to comment, during one of his abusive rants, while hunting desperately for any missile to hurl at Steiner, that it was no coincidence that Steiner's best friends were the two most senior men in the complex. Steiner had seen this as Boris's jealousy at not being invited, and being discomforted by this thought rather than at Boris's accusation, admitted to himself that he had deliberately excluded Boris: his presence would disturb the precious dynamics of these dinner-parties that he particularly treasured. In contrast, he looked forward to introducing his friends to Sabine. He was proud of her and wanted to show her off.

When the time came, he saw that Sabine was nervous and he sought to put her at ease.

"I think you'll like them, they're both eccentric but that's as far as any comparison goes. They're not to be afraid of."

Sabine smiled. "Three professors. Why should I be afraid?"

Steiner had long outgrown awareness of his status and was surprised by this remark. She spoke with pride, he decided, and he was flattered and a little humbled. She pressed him for a description of the two professors and their wives. Steiner frowned in concentration.

"Hirsch is dry, sarcastic, ironical, honest, sincere, sad, remorseful for his many sins..."

"God in heaven! Is he a party member or a Catholic?"

Steiner shook his head but relented at her laughter. "It's difficult; Hirsch is complicated."

"You haven't answered my question."

"Neither. Emphatically not either."

"Then what makes him act as both? What are his sins?"

"Sins of the mind – young girls with shapely legs – they torment him."

Sabine nodded. "And his wife has short legs and thick ankles."

"I don't know how you knew that – about the ankles."

Sabine stretched out her legs, pulled up her slacks to contemplate her own slim ankles, and looked at Steiner so coyly that they both burst into laughter.

"And I'm supposed to like this man? What's she like, the wife?"

"Ulrika is a chemist; brilliant mind although you wouldn't guess it from her conversation. I suppose because she's socially ill at ease she makes awkward small-talk."

"I'm not surprised. Being married to a man who resents her can't make her feel good about herself."

Steiner studied Sabine thoughtfully. "He does resent her. He tries not to, but in his heart he blames her for a marriage that has emasculated him and robbed him of his freedom. But I didn't tell you that. How did you know?"

She smiled. "In a former life I was burnt at the stake. A great cruelty but perhaps not wholly undeserved." She spoke steadily and her smile was so inscrutable that Steiner was not certain that she was joking. "And the Schellenbergs?"

"Complicated again. They lost a child many years ago. It killed them inside. But it's strange – when you meet them separately you can glimpse them as they were. Once they were turbulently in love. They were an unlikely couple, differing profoundly in beliefs. They would argue passionately, often bitterly, in festering rows that would last for days – sincere spirited people, tormented by the hurt they caused each other, but unable to give way on matters that compromised their beliefs."

"That was then. What about now?"

"They are peculiarly kind to each other. I say peculiarly because I've never seen it to such an extreme. It's touching but also sad."

"Guilt. They are trying to reassure each other against the guilt each knows the other feels."

Steiner stared at her in surprise. "Exactly that – you still have your powers; they evidently forgot to burn your broomstick."

"I think you think women know very little."

Steiner smiled. "You're too polite. You mean I'm patronising, and of course you're right."

Sabine considered this. "And you're right too, about being too polite. I don't like to argue. I don't know where it will end. Besides, it's only natural for you; you're used to people knowing less than you."

Steiner considered this for a moment. "I hope I don't do that. I don't feel I do."

She looked away from him as if suddenly shy. "It doesn't matter so much. You're a*Muffelchen anyhow."

They laughed and this moment fixed, 'Muffelchen' as her pet name for him.

Steiner reached the end of the avenue of lights. The switching station was before him. It was comforting to find the place almost unchanged. To do so accepted the possibility that the time associated with this place could be rediscovered. But on closer inspection he saw that not all was untouched by time. The twisted matrix of grey transformers and cooling pipes was corroded in places and the ground was inundated with white-flowering weeds.

Sabine took over the arrangements for the dinner-party, spending the day cooking in spite of Steiner's protestations. His guests were used to simple food and he was afraid that

---

* A little sourpuss

such a grand meal would spoil the informality of the occasion.

But his fears were unfounded: Sabine was not only the perfect hostess but appeared remarkably at ease. It seemed to Steiner that she was far from being overwhelmed by the professors and their wives. In fact it was Hirsch who seemed not his usual self.

Hirsch was a tall, well-built man. Middle age had slowed his step and hunched his shoulders but he retained the developed physique of a former athlete. He had the face of a mathematician. His nose was large but finely shaped. His pale fleshy lips were capable only of a weak smile that appeared peculiarly dishonest in contrast to his otherwise evident sincerity. His eyes, behind owl-like spectacles, were faded blue. In repose his expression was slightly sad, but the dry cutting delivery for which he was renowned was softened by an impish gleam of humour around the mouth and eyes that was almost as disconcerting as his extreme directness.

During the meal, Hirsch ate in silence, which was unusual; normally he would hold forth on any topic that he knew to be provocative. Steiner recognised the symptoms: Hirsch was shy. This was a revelation; he had never known Hirsch to be shy. And this altered dynamic encouraged his perpetually nervous wife, Ulrika, to become so garrulous that Steiner had to stop himself from staring at her in amazement.

Unlike her husband, Ulrika's appearance was entirely contradictory to both her occupation and her intellect. She had the figure of a peasant, strong and thickset, bred to work the land. Her hair was dark and coarse but her features were sharp and her fingers fine and clever. Her nervous jabbering speech was trivial. The only clue to her intelligence was her sharp eyes, which darted nervously around avoiding contact with others. She praised the meal with genuine appreciation. Sabine smiled at her with such warmth and pleasure that Steiner was surprised to observe how Ulrika held her gaze and returned her smile; and her gabbled conversation slowed as if that smile had calmed and reassured her.

It seemed to Steiner that Sabine's presence cast a spell on the gathering. Even the Schellenbergs were affected, and this was a surprise to Steiner. Schellenberg was usually so absorbed in his science that he seemed entirely oblivious to anything outside it. He was apparently a more extreme caricature of his profession than Hirsch; physically he was small and wizened but with a wiry energy about him rather than the frailty suggested by his straggling white hair. His eyes were dark and sunken. At a casual glance he looked some years older than Hirsch, but when animated, there was a suggestion of youth in the brightness of his eyes, eagerness of his expression and the rounded contours of his face. Such animation was usually excited by a discussion of his passion: pure physics. But tonight he engaged in the small talk around the dinner table with rare enthusiasm. His wife watched him with an almost maternal pleasure.

Steiner's description of Sylvie Schellenberg had been incomplete. She was a handsome robust straightforward woman with the ruddy complexion of a countrywoman. Like Hirsch she did not hold back on strong opinions but unlike him she had a rare quality of not giving offence.

Sabine refilled the guests' wineglasses before they were empty. During the meal she enjoined with Ulrika in teasing Hirsch. Steiner was concerned that the apparently good-humoured malice had a sharpness that could easily sour. Hirsch was a difficult man and in company with his wife, ancient and painful accusations were easily resurrected. But Hirsch seemed unusually cowed and allowed his wife's teasing with good humour. Steiner was pleased at the evident rapport between Ulrika and Sabine that defied his private prediction. Hirsch and Ulrika were socially dysfunctional, engulfed in their private enmity that emanated from Hirsch's irritation with his wife, and divided them from normal social intercourse. It was Sylvie Schellenberg whom he had expected Sabine to warm to. Sylvie's straightforward sincerity could usually be relied upon to win her over to her own sex; and yet, as Steiner glanced over at Sylvie with this thought in his mind, he saw that she watched Sabine contemplatively. Sylvie, more than any of them, was astute. He wondered what she was thinking and observed that he had not seen Sabine talk to her or even look at her during the course of the meal.

As was usual, the conversation took a serious turn and for Hirsch and the Schellenbergs this was an evident relief from the strain of small talk. Schellenberg remarked sourly that his application for experimental time on a particle accelerator in the Soviet Union had been rejected, his supposition being that research in the area of pure physics took second place to those with a military application. Hirsch could not miss the opportunity for a jibe.

"So even party members don't get their way all the time."

Schellenberg had no understanding of irony, or indeed any form of language that was not strictly literal, and so, even though he had known Hirsch for so many years, he took this remark more seriously than was justified by its intent.

"That's a tiresome cut, Hirsch. I had little choice in my position as you know very well."

Hirsch pulled on his pipe. "Exactly my point – career advancement."

Schellenberg bristled with a rare petulance. "I suppose I should be used to you after all these years, Hirsch, but there are times when your nonsense annoys me. You know that's not true."

Hirsch smiled uneasily. Confrontation was second nature to him. He never took offence himself – far from it, he took great pleasure in personal affront, the more insulting the better – and never ceased to be surprised when others did. And by some peculiar obstinacy of nature, the apology that formed in his heart (behind his rudeness he was mortified at the thought of causing hurt) manifested itself as a further insult:

"Well I can't see any other reason – unless of course you've been hiding your admiration for Herr Ulbricht?"

And Schellenberg, failing to understand the motivation for this remark, was for once seriously annoyed.

"I rather resent that. You're so proud of being the most senior non-party man, but that itself is a conceit – and it doesn't make the rest of us hypocrites."

Hirsch busied himself re-lighting his pipe. "Not if you believe in it, of course."

Schellenberg pulled his wrist gently away from his wife's restraining hand, where she had been holding it between her thumb and finger, as if checking his pulse for some increase in heart rate that could be harmful to him. He shook his head uneasily.

"You are, as always, Hirsch, the voice of my conscience. Perhaps that's why you anger me sometimes – because there is of course some truth in what you say. You know my opinions very well – and you know my doubts. I'm not political in the way that you are, but I'm a socialist by conscience. My only affinity for capitalism is democracy; I'd like to be able to vote off most of the Politburo – most of the S.E.D. for that matter – but I wouldn't replace them with Erhard or Kiesinger, or even another Adenauer, for that matter. I think the underground in both Germanies deceive themselves. It's as impossible to be a communist in the Federal Republic as it is to be a democrat in the Democratic Republic." He smiled suddenly, his good-humour restored. "That's my solution: let them have our capitalists and we'll have their communists. There – how about that? Then we'll all be happy."

Steiner laughed. "You'd make such an appalling politician, Schellenberg – you just want everyone to be happy. That won't do at all; you'll start another revolution with ideas like that."

Hirsch was not prepared to let the subject be changed. "But this is nonsense. You talk about the underground deceiving themselves – it's you that deceive yourself: you can't compare losing out on a promotion to being run in by the STASI."

Schellenberg frowned and opened his mouth to protest but Sylvie interrupted firmly:

"That's enough – the two of you. Quarrelling about science is bad enough, but politics..." She shook her head. Ulrika laughed nervously. Steiner chose this break in the atmosphere to refill the empty glasses. Sabine appeared to have forgotten her role as hostess. She stared in silence at the empty seat opposite her. Steiner's movement in refilling her glass appeared to awaken her from some reverie.

"My father was in the MIS." Steiner was struck by some strangeness about her. Her voice was cold, factual, defiant, and this, with her smile, gave him the impression that she made this dramatic announcement with pride. He was puzzled by the intentness of her concentration on the empty place opposite her. Steiner met Sylvie's puzzled eyes for a moment. Schellenberg rescued the silence that threatened awkwardness. He looked at Sabine with an expression that was both grave and kindly.

"I think with our history there are few of us without some shameful connection. Today it is the STASI. Once at least they were the reliable sons and daughters of the victims of fascism."

Hirsch gave a short dismissive laugh. "The trouble with you, Schellenberg, is that your brain is so filled with the contemplation of sub-atomic particles that it leaves no space for any thought that wouldn't disgrace a six-year-old."

Schellenberg shook his head indulgently. "Ah – now you're insulting me – and that, according to my wife, means that I must be winning the argument."

They all laughed and Steiner observed to Schellenberg. "And now you've made him laugh – ask Sylvie what that means." He turned to Sabine, disconcerted by her abstraction. "That is one of Hirsch's more amiable characteristics: he is not offended by a joke at his expense. But Schellenberg is right. Shameful connections you said, but in truth the pair of you can afford such a discussion. That is the privilege of the Jews. For me it is different. My father was, as you know, a Nazi, and not just one who was swept along with it; he believed in it, and when confronted with the *evil of it, he would grudgingly admit to 'some excesses', but there were a thousand excuses in his heart that denied his words."*

Steiner felt a hand under the table slip into his. He turned to Sabine. Her eyes met his briefly before turning back to the empty place opposite her. He watched her for a moment, concerned by the inappropriate smile she directed into space, so that he missed a beat in the conversation. Schellenberg was speaking again:

"Besides, the tyranny of Stalin is the disgrace of one man, not a system."

Hirsch shook his head dismisively. "Rubbish, What sort of a system allows a maniac to lead it? And in any case, Lenin was going the same way if death hadn't done the decent thing for his reputation."

Sylvie laughed. "I wonder if you believe in anything you say, Hirsch. I fancy not, since you never agree with anybody about anything. I think you are like a western politician in opposition. God help us if mathematicians come to power." Steiner observed that Sabine's attention had returned to the table; she watched Sylvie intently.

Hirsch looked pleased. "Well I'll confound you. I share your husband's affinity for Marx – and not just because the great tyrant was such a poor disciple. He was cynical for a communist – Marx that is. He understood that the greatest danger came from his colleagues, but understood, too, man's greed and its satisfaction by capitalism."

Sylvie frowned. "Did I read an edited version of Das Kapital? Or did he not predict that capitalism would destroy itself?"

Hirsch smiled dryly. "And so it will, but communism first. Our system is superior in every respect – who can argue with social justice? Its problem is that it deals with humanity as it ought to be rather than how it is – and because it can't lower its gaze from the heavens, so it will be destroyed from the ground.

Ulrika took a large gulp of wine as if to bolster her

courage. "Thus spoke the prophet." She darted a smile at Sabine. "I hope you won't be reporting us, Sabine."

They all laughed but Steiner observed that Sabine remained uncomfortable at the turn of the conversation. He felt a childish satisfaction – pleased that she was witness to the freedom of expression that he shared with his friends. She would know that such talk carried extreme danger without complete trust. Was it his imagination or was there some hint of envy as well as fear at this conversation?

Schellenberg sighed. "We live in troubled times. I will admit to being grateful to be so absorbed in my work. There have been times in my life..." He hesitated, blinked across the table. "Well you know my story. Time was..." He left the sentence unfinished which was characteristic of Schellenberg: his mind often left his speech behind. His wife, following the direction of his thoughts, stroked his arm tenderly. Steiner saw that she darted a glance at Sabine and wondered at the peculiar behaviour of the two towards each other; particularly Sylvie whom he had only ever known to be direct and straightforward. Sabine appeared unaware of this brief scrutiny; unaware even of the conversation around her, staring into the empty space opposite her with an odd half-smile fixed upon her face.

The party broke up. Schellenberg professed to be tired, although his wife embarrassed him by saying that this would not stop him from spending half the night working. Steiner arose with his guests from the table. Sabine appeared not to notice. Her eyes raised slowly from the space opposite her. She nodded her head imperceptibly as if in agreement with some unheard remark and her expression displayed hauteur and arrogance. Steiner was embarrassed; she was entirely changed from the graceful hostess. He recognised this mood: the temptress abandoned to the heat of the dance, surrounded by a harem of entranced men ruled by her disdain. She recovered herself sufficiently to make polite farewells. Steiner saw the Schellenbergs to the door, amused at Schellenberg's impatience to be on his way; knowing the truth of Sylvie's remark: his work beckoned irresistibly.

Sylvie lingered at the door, her eyes darting towards the sound of voices in the dining room. Her eyes met with Steiners' for a moment and she opened her mouth to speak, but the voices drew near. She returned her attention to Steiner, pursed her lips and shook her head quickly, significantly and furtively, before turning away.

Steiner stared after her, startled. He wondered what it was Sylvie had wanted to say before she was interrupted. The message of her shake of the head was clear: she disapproved of Sabine.

Steiner closed the door behind Hirsch and Ulrika with unease. Sylvie was a good-natured woman, quick to understand and slow to condemn. What was it that had provoked this extreme and uncharacteristic reaction?

Sabine squatted by the fire, surveying the flames, her forward-leaning figure an effigy of intensity. She drained the last of a bottle of wine into her glass. Steiner sat in a chair by her side.

"It went well I thought."

She answered the question behind his words. "Good people; nice intelligent, thoughtful people." Her eyes met his with a crooked smile. She moved to sit at his feet, watching him, close but at a distance like a female cat curled up enjoying the sensuality of physical closeness that an outstretched stroking hand would spoil. Steiner respected her deliberate distance against his desire to sit with her with his arm around her waist.

"Are all your friends older than you?"

Steiner considered. "My friends here, yes. My work – as Boris so often reminded me – is not the new science, and the people go with it."

"You know why Boris said those things?"

"His views are not unusual. Who's to say they're wrong? I just think he accepts too readily..."

"No." Sabine rose to her feet and leant against the fireplace, facing him. "No – whatever he believed, he would

deny you; he is deeply, bitterly envious of you. Do you not know that?"

Steiner frowned in confusion, He remembered his suspicion that Boris had used debate to impress Sabine but this was something different. He protested:

"That doesn't make sense. It's Boris who has all the prospects, being his age and being in such a field, whereas I – I am the caretaker of a science he believes to be redundant."

Sabine smiled. "False modesty."

"No. If what you say is right, then he sees me very differently to how I see myself."

"He is nothing compared to you and he knows it. He would rant on to me, mocking your views, trying to impress me with his own, but he didn't deceive me for a moment. He is bitterly envious of you." She smiled. "I think having that knowledge about you intrigued me long before I met you."

Steiner considered. "If you are right, and I'm not convinced, perhaps he feels insecure. I mean – if you betrayed how you felt, it must have tormented him."

Sabine drained her glass and raised it. "I want to get drunk."

Steiner got up obediently to fetch more wine, troubled by her mood, trying to find words in his mind for the disturbance it aroused: reckless, dangerous, triumphant, out of control – mad – that was it – not completely, but not quite sane. He found a bottle of wine open in the kitchen and returned. He would have preferred not to give it to her; she was already drunk. He was arrested by the sound of her voice and stopped by the door. She was directly in his line of sight through the crack of the open door between the hinges. Her eyes were raised, focussing into space, her expression animated. Her tone mocked. "Talk for me – laugh for me. Such nice intelligent people – so shy without you, so uncomfortable – without comfort – com-fort." She turned away. Steiner caught her expression and was shocked by her agitation. He stood frozen, missing the moment to re-enter the room. Sabine turned again to face across the fireplace. He saw her raise her eyes, saw the return of spirit to her features, but spirit without pride or arrogance – naïve, simple and honest like a child reassured by a parent after some failure it has taken unnecessarily to heart. "They couldn't know – they saw a young woman, tall, taller than any of them, and careless – care-less – couldn't care less – watching all the time for a husband chasing young skirts – and to lose a child – what do I care for that?" *She giggled and the noise sounded hysterical to Steiner.* "Lose a child – how careless – careless – careless, I think."

Steiner re-entered the room. Her eyes turned towards him and changed expression so rapidly that he questioned to himself if he had imagined their former expression. Now they were unfocussed and vague as if only half-aware of his presence. Her attention was taken with the wine. Steiner let her take the bottle, reluctant to pour it into her glass, evading the responsibility. She looked at him knowingly and filled the glass to the brim, drank most of it in one gulp, drew herself to her full height and smiled mockingly and defiantly.

"Now that I'm drunk, I can tell you the truth: she didn't like me – the Schellenberg woman."

"You need to be drunk to tell the truth?"

"You don't deny it because you know I'm right."

Steiner poured himself a glass of wine. "The empty chair opposite you – was it your friend, Maria sitting there – the one you talk to when you are alone?"

Sabine nodded her head slowly. "Did you think I was confident and self-assured? Is that how I seemed to you?"

"Yes."

She laughed. "People think that." *She smiled as if at some inner amusement.* "But she saw – the Schellenberg woman – and she didn't like me. You saw that. My last lover – before Boris I mean – his sister hated me."

Steiner looked away from her in troubled silence; he was shocked, not so much by her words but by her complacency, as if this knowledge was somehow reassuring to her. Her

52

expression softened, caressing him with her gaze, her eyes smiling into his, and he was disconcerted by this searching intimacy that examined his private thoughts. She turned away and a moment later the silence was broken by the chiming tune of her locket. He stared at her bowed neck. There was something macabre about that mechanical tune and yet he felt irresistibly drawn to it. It was a part of the strangeness about her that separated her world from his and that he was attracted to as a doomed rat to the tune of the Pied Piper. He was suddenly afraid of everything; of the unnatural pace of this relationship, of the inexorable change in the rhythm of his life but above all, of the strength of his emotions.

He led her upstairs. She was suddenly drunk and sleepy. He sensed that this was an act to forestall any sexual advance by him. She sat on the bed, turned away from him. He stared at her bent, forlorn back, and felt a catch at his heart at the thought of how precious she was to him, and how, without her, he would be desolate and alone, just as Boris.

He kissed her gently on the forehead and stood by the window; he lit a cigarette and listened to the rhythm of her breathing. His senses were heightened. The cigarette tasted different, with a pungency and fragrance he had not experienced since adolescence. He was elated. He would leave her asleep, go out into the night to the dance hall and dance until dawn, returning while she was still asleep. But this elation was tainted by some trouble associated with her: an intimation that her feelings towards him were equivocal. He turned on a whim and was surprised to see that her eyes were open, surveying him thoughtfully – sober and wide awake, exposing the deceit of her apparent sleepiness. He turned away again and finished his cigarette, but now the air of the room was oppressive and he opened the window to let in the night air and noises.

The window looked out across a walled alley that connected the gardens behind the apartments; and beyond it, moonlit pastures stretched towards a haze of light in the distance that hung over Magedeburg. A chorus of grasshoppers bleated from the grasslands. A black cat stalked noiselessly up the alley, skirting the shadows up to an unbroken patch of moonlight. He jumped up onto the wall as if the jagged margin separating light from dark was an impenetrable barrier, and continued his measured prowl, sweeping his long tail in perfect time with the delicate march of his paws. Steiner watched the creature with pleasure, oblivious in his engrossment for some time to another noise: a chattering unintelligible murmur from within the room. He turned to see Sabine lying on her side, one hand outstretched, the other across her forehead, her head rocking from side to side as if in pain. Her lips trembled. Her muttering passed in and out of intelligibility like an out of range radio transmission.

"Far too late now – catch me – set her free – please, please – let her rest now – didn't hurt her – beat her – tell him to stop – she's alive – gone – wouldn't do it – can't listen – can't listen."

Steiner crossed the room. She writhed in her dreams, and then, as if disturbed by his presence, she sat up, her arms punching towards him as if defending herself against him. Her eyes were open but unseeing, or so he thought, and then one arm stretched towards him, unclasping, beckoning. Her eyes smiled with recognition, unsurprised, as if he had been with her in her dreams. Her hand clasped his; her fingers worked in between his.

"You were talking in your sleep," he said.

Her eyes met his; her voice was a whisper. "I love you."

Steiner was distracted by the humming of the transformers. The heat from the coils distorted the night air, causing it to refract, creating an illusion of movement in the convoluted grey pipe-work. An image formed in the shimmering air, towering above the switching station: a moving figure dancing in the darkness of night to the beat of dance-music, taunting him as she snaked towards an unseen partner, her smile as twisted as the pipe-work.

Steiner visited Boris the following day. His friend had stopped visiting due to the presence of Sabine and by unspoken agreement, Steiner had become the visitor.

Boris was drunk, as seemed usual now, and in a sullen bitter temper. Steiner tried to avoid speaking of Sabine but it was only a matter of minutes before Boris turned to the subject that obsessed him.

"I've been thinking about that last night. I told you how little she must think of herself to try and pacify me in that way – but I see it now – what a fool she made of me; she wasn't pacifying me but humiliating me. I remember that look on her face. She was laughing at me, and I didn't understand – conceited fool. Even now I flush in shame at the thought of it."

Steiner was moved by his friend's anguish. Only the night before he had imagined what it would mean to him to lose her. He remembered the surprise and relief he had felt at those whispered words; he heard them now – "I love you" – and pitied his friend. He was aroused from his thoughts by the intensity of Boris' gaze and changed the subject as if to divert Boris from divining his thoughts.

"Did she ever talk to you of her friend, Maria?"

"The wonderful, accomplished, beautiful, brilliant Maria? Does she talk of anything else?"

"Talks of – and talks to I suspect, even when she isn't there."

Boris looked pained. His voice was hushed to a whisper. "Yes – she does that."

"Actually I wonder if she exists."

Boris looked perplexed. "How do you mean?"

"Well, for example, one day last week I came home and found two empty wine glasses. I went to wash them and the rim of one was covered with the brightest red lipstick I've ever seen. I teased her about it, asked her if she'd been entertaining one of the wives of our Russian friends. She told me that Maria had visited, that I'd just missed her. It seems strange that I always just miss her. It's like a trick in a

detective novel: lipstick on a glass, or a cigarette in an ashtray that's still smoking. And she gave me the strangest look."

"You mean you've never met her?" Steiner shook his head and Boris looked perplexed. "Well that is strange. She exists all right, larger than life – and I can guess why she gave you a strange look: because you almost guessed the truth. She is not one of our friend's wives, but she is a Russian – a Don Cossack, she will tell you, with a look on her face to put a mere Teuton in his rightful place."

Steiner wondered if it were chance or design that he had not met Maria, but asked aloud:

And is she wonderful and brilliant and all of those things?"

Boris looked sour. "That and more – a party activist for starters - but deadly. I admit to being biased. I have no love for 'La Maria'."

"A femme fatale?"

"It's hard to know who's the leader and who the follower; they make a truly dreadful double-act. We went out together one night. Oddly enough it was to a party of Russian officers and wives – a grand affair at the Interhotel in Magdeburg. It was a two-woman-show, and I do mean a show. They wore the same dresses – black ball-gowns with gold braid. They danced all night with each other: the most outrageous dancing, as if they were – you know – together. The men couldn't take their eyes off them. And as for the women – I've never seen such a display of bared gold teeth."

Steiner laughed and Boris smiled for the first time. He sighed. "They were magnificent, I admit, but if I have one piece of advice for you, it is this: never, ever be with them together. They will compete with each other to belittle you. They are like two schoolgirls, whispering together, every joke at your expense. And Maria is bitter about men. In that way she is the leader. She boasts about her mistreatment of men, and Sabine admires her for it, and tries to outdo her. That night was the most shameful of my life. I wanted to leave her;

worse than that, I wanted to hit her – to hurt her in the only way I knew how. It is the closest I have ever been to hitting a woman. I did it in my mind – struck her across the face with my fist closed, watched her fall to the ground with her lip split open and her blood pouring out. But what did I do? I took it all with a smile as if I didn't care. I regret that. I wish above all things that I had walked out on her that night – but I didn't have the strength."

Boris gulped half a glass of Vodka and swilled it in his mouth with an expression of distaste as if at some bitter but vital medicine. He glanced awkwardly for a brief moment at Steiner before turning away. His voice was a hoarse whisper.

"Does she ever talk of me?"

Steiner pitied his friend, knowing the cost to his pride of this question. He felt himself flush at the memory of his conversation with her about Boris. He chose to lie and was appalled at the falseness in his voice.

"No, not to me."

Boris nodded as if expecting this reply. He shifted uneasily. "The telephone rang yesterday. I went to answer it but there was no one there."

Steiner understood the question he was being asked. Boris's face was a mask of impassivity but the clasping and unclasping of his right hand betrayed him.

Steiner kept his voice casual. "Yesterday – she was with me. We both finished early and walked back together. What time was this?"

"Late afternoon just before dark. You would have been home by then. Its just that..." Now he could no longer contain his embarrassment. "It was that time – I didn't connect it at first: she would telephone me then – just before dark on a Friday. I never knew why. When we first met, she would call and we would talk as friends do. Then, later on, it would be to make an arrangement to meet. And then, when things weren't right, she would still call, sometimes without anything to say. I wondered more than once why she had called. And one day the coincidence struck me: I was sitting by the telephone,

watching the shadow of a table on the floor in front of me, and was struck by the familiarity of absent-mindedly watching that shadow, always in the same place, and the fading light through the window, and I worked backwards, placing the days she had called. They were nearly always the same: on a Friday."

Steiner was intrigued. "You never asked her about it?"

"No. It was coming to an end by then; but still she called. Sometimes she would ask coldly how I was, as if she were compelled to call against her will, had some need to hear my voice but was angry with me at the humiliation it caused her. And then, at the end, the phone would ring – just like yesterday – and there would be no one there."

This conversation intrigued and troubled Steiner. He didn't doubt Boris. He had always known his friend to be truthful, and besides, he lacked the imagination to invent such a story. This doubt, once aroused, would not dissipate. He confronted Sabine that evening. He had rehearsed his speech. He would tell her, apparently casually, what Boris had said. But as he sat with her, she seemed uneasy. Was it his imagination, or had he somehow alerted her to his doubts? He changed his tactics, guiltily aware of the mistrust that caused him to do so. He would give her no time to construct or evade. He blurted out:

"Boris says you rang him yesterday."

She frowned. "Boris?" She got up from her seat alongside him, apparently casually, to reach for the locket she had left on a dresser. Steiner had lost the element of surprise. She turned the locket over in her hands, opened the lid and listened to the chimes with a half-smile of pleasure, as if the tune was new to her. Her reply was low, flat and absent-minded, as if the matter was unimportant to her. "I'm sorry for what I did to him. It should never have happened. It was a mistake."

"So you didn't telephone him?" She shook her head and looked him directly in the eyes. "No. I wouldn't call Boris – not now. What am I supposed to have said to him?"

Steiner was embarrassed. "The phone rang off when he answered it. He thought it was you."

She lowered her head, apparently intent on the chiming tune from the locket. Her hair fell over her face, exposing her long slender neck. She looked up suddenly with wide childlike eyes.

"You don't trust me, do you?"

Steiner was confused. She had given the answer she would have given if innocent of the accusation, but she had given herself time to think, as if alert to the danger of a trap. And that very awareness made him doubt her.

"I had to ask. I've known Boris some years. I've never known him to be a liar."

"So then I must be?" She glanced at him and he was surprised by her expression. He was expecting wounded pride or hurt, but she smiled. Just as after the dinner-party, it seemed to him that her emotions were inappropriate; she was satisfied, as if re-assured by his distrust of her; only this time there was some other quality in her smile: mocking and triumphant; she was laughing at him.

Steiner's thoughts were interrupted by the sensation of a vibration against his body. He looked down to see his hand shaking with a fine tremor. He watched it with detached curiosity, understanding that this was the physical manifestation of that distant trouble. He made no attempt to still the uncontrolled limb and watched its tremor increase in magnitude. It was as if this twitching limb was tied in time to that awful past, mimicking the disturbance of his mind at those events. The sensation became unpleasant and he stilled the tremor with an effort of will. The pale white hand, indistinct in the pre-dawn light, lay lifeless; in his imagination, a fluttering bird, mortally wounded, its life-blood drained.

He rose to his feet, grateful for the distant haze of amber from beyond the horizon, dispelling the fears of the night: of restless re-awakened dreams.

He headed for home, re-entering the avenue. Now the halos from the lights were distinct, but he was watchful, suspecting this place of preparing another trick for him. His steps grew cautious. Some mischievous power seemed to interfere playfully with the echo of his tread – now soft and shuffling in front of him, then loud and distorted behind him. He stopped and turned, but could not catch the echo out: it stopped as he stopped. He turned and carried on. In the distance at the far end of the avenue, a light wind whipped up a small pile of leaves. He watched with concentration; the pattern seemed extraordinarily regular as if a miniature slow-moving tornado was fixed to the spot, spinning the leaves slowly over. And then he smiled as he grew nearer and understood the deception: these were not leaves, but a troupe of performing mice, pirouetting in perfect time, tumbling over each other, somersaulting with comic seriousness in their twitching whiskers and beady black eyes. He sighed. This was a magic place. He knew that he only had to shake his head and the mice would be gone. But he didn't want them to go, and kept himself perfectly still until at last the little creatures turned once again into swirling leaves. He turned away with a sigh of disappointment. But his mood had changed. He felt her presence, knew that she was near now. The time approached when she would announce her presence to him. His anticipation grew as he neared home.

The alleys leading to the back of his apartment were hung with dark shadows against the first grey light. The magical feeling persisted. He had the strangest feeling that this place, so physically unchanged, could switch in a moment with the past, into her time. He stood on the threshold. One step could take him into it. He paused. Had it already happened? That was how these things happened in stories: you waited for the moment, thinking it hadn't happened, and then found that it had – you were in a dream, somewhere else – dead. All was still, all was poised; one breath would blow him into that other time. He listened. The silence changed. He knew what was to happen. The first musical note was followed by a long silence, so that he wondered if he had imagined it, and then, from the darkness of the passageways, came the chiming tune of her locket.

The tune grew fainter as if the bearer of the locket had turned away, and then it was louder again, as if it had turned in the darkness, rushing towards him, more powerful than ever he remembered it, infused with a deeper melody. His heart was stirred to a new reality; all his senses were alive to the change: the fragrance of the air, a tinge of blue in the light of the stars, the pulse of blood in his veins, the power in his muscles at rest.

She stood before him, her head bowed, her attention drawn to the locket and engrossed in its tune. They had spent the evening at the Hirsches'. It had been a pleasant evening. Sabine had been relaxed. Hirsch had been in good humour; his caustic wit turned on the tyranny of capital instead of his wife, for a change. Sabine had joined with Ulrika in accusing him of espousing Schellenberg's political beliefs. A lively but good-humoured debate had followed.

Sabine's lips moved as if in a trance. "When little girls are young, their fathers, sometimes their mothers, read them bed-time stories to help them sleep. My father was in this way like other fathers. When I was a little girl, only just old enough to understand simple language, I learnt before my age a dreadful vocabulary. When it came to bed-time, I would try to hide by staying quiet in a corner in the hope that I would be overlooked; it happened occasionally that I was left in peace with my mother and little sister; but most nights the time would come – the same awful words: 'Well, young lady it's past your bed time.' And my teeth would chatter in my head, and my mother would shake her head as she kissed me good night, with an expression that said: 'What a queer child.' And I would have my bed time story – obscene nightmares that would lurk in the darkness of my room on leashes until sleep set them free. I've told you my father was in the M.I.S. but not that he was a STASI interrogator. His stories were of his day's work. Work!" She laughed – a harsh musical sound, but with real amusement. "A woman whose husband had been arrested and they wanted to know more of his crimes – I remember those stories. I remember because I can't forget them. He told me because it pleased him to see me shaking with fear, wetting myself sometimes. No, not, pleased him; it gave him some twisted relief to tell me. He would savour some particular obscenity in its most intimate perverted detail. And the greatest obscenity of all: it relieved his conscience; even he was human; even he suffered some trouble of heart which was relieved by these outpourings to his infant daughter.

They drove one woman mad so that she would babble nonsense, but even in her derangement his presence would send her into a frenzy; he was proud of that: that he had the power to penetrate her madness. That power elevated him above the human." She was silent for a moment. "Above the human – yes – I think that lived in him alongside his deepest inadequacy – an explanation perhaps for his inability to relate normally to others. He had a particular hatred for the people he worked with: they were too coarse for him, they did not share his sensibilities. That grotesque twisted madman loved music – not the simple common tunes, but classical, instrumental and choral – particularly choral. I remember once – he would sit in his chair, his particular favourite chair that he would not allow anyone else to sit in, drawn up in a dark corner of the room, unlit so that on a dark day you could be unsure if he were there or not – and this particular time I didn't know he was there. Music was playing – Verdi's Requiem. In the dark recess of that corner, I caught a gleam of something bright. I strained my eyes, wondering what it was – and I remember my shock at the realisation of his presence. The gleam of light was from the water in his eyes; he was crying; tears streamed down his cheeks from the beauty of that music.

And I remember the horrific story he told me that night. It was only years after that I guessed at the connection. The sickness of his mind relished in the violation of any finer emotions that flourished in his corrupt soul. That was what moved him to acts of special brutality. The night I speak of he told me of a mother, beaten beyond endurance in an attempt to extract a denouncement of her adolescent son. But he was defied by a mother's supreme love for her child. It mystified and enraged him. He tormented her with his own hands after his lackeys had finished with her, with unbelievable cruelty, just as a sadistic little boy torments some small creature. Mercifully she died and he was denied. I remember my relief at the knowledge that her suffering was over. He was frenzied. Had she lived, he would have dissected her living brain in search of the mechanism that loved her child above all the torments he could devise. That was his justification: that he was a philosopher, a philanthropist, examining the human spirit. But in truth he was a sadist, embittered and enraged by any emotion that he could not corrupt, crushing it with violent contempt." She paused in contemplation. "And yet that madman was moved to tears by his music. He talked about that woman for a long time afterwards; about the unsurpassable love of a mother for a child, as if he had learnt some valuable wisdom that he was proud of and boasted of to his own child. He was, above all, conceited.

"But then he was confounded again, this time by two young lovers: she, a beautiful fair girl of Polish blood; and he, her opposite, a dark-eyed gypsy with rings in his ears – rings that were ripped off, shredding his poor ears. And their love surpassed all his torments. I remember the confusion in his eyes, the wounded affront as he said: 'She had only to admit to his crimes and she would have been spared. I gave her my word.' Perhaps that was what wounded him: that she must have doubted his precious word to defy him. Her love was not an explanation he could understand. I remember a vision I created of that woman; it has come to me many times since – awake and in nightmares; I remember my thoughts and have wondered at the precociousness of them: how easy it would have been for her to misunderstand the passion and

rapture in those evil eyes intent on hers at the moment when the flame of life flickered and was extinguished; how that light in his eyes was her last image on this earth: a false beacon in that dark passage." She laughed again, this time without amusement. "The thoughts of a young girl, inspired by that unnatural puzzlement. And there were others who must have seen beyond it to the contempt that mocked them.

"There was another he tortured: a middle-aged doctor. Instead of desperate fear, pleading with him for her life, she was outraged. He described her reaction as that of a strict governess who had caught a young boy peering up her skirt. It aroused him to a frenzy that I recognised with a knowledge way beyond my years as sexual. He delighted in her outrage, assaulting her repeatedly to provoke it. He told me of his anger when she died, and how he had the corpse tied to a chair to relish that expression that was frozen on her dead face."

Steiner's emotions were a mixture of horror, anger and pity, not just for these distant victims, but for the poor child that had been their witness. But, overwhelming all, he felt alienated from the young woman before him, separated from him by this dreadful knowledge, and he felt ashamed of the injustice of this irrational emotion.

"Sometimes he would reprieve a prisoner, not because his crime was minor, quite the reverse – it would be one who had committed a real crime rather one of the falsely charged innocents. He would let that one go, not out of mercy but to demonstrate his power to redeem as well as condemn – to give life as well as death." She lapsed into silence. He could only guess at the horrors that occupied her thoughts, so that it was a surprise when she spoke and her words indicated her consciousness of the present. "I've never told anyone before."

Steiner wanted to reassure her. He took her hand awkwardly in his and squeezed it, relieved by the answering pressure. He had feared that this dreadful confession would remove her from him. He spoke the first words that came into his mind, fearful of the silence that would take her from him.

"I knew there was something, without knowing what it was."

She smiled. "There was, as you say, something."

"It explains many things – why you talk in your sleep, your hatred of shadows: you cannot sit in a room without all the lights on and you always position yourself in the middle of the floor."

She squeezed his hand. "I didn't know it was so obvious."

He smiled into her eyes that were sometimes so artful, but now so innocent. "Do you still see him there, watching you from the shadows?"

She nodded. "Strange that of all those terrors I should be most haunted by one that was really nothing: seeing him there when I thought I was alone. It's true: I still check the shadows, half-expecting him to be there. He had that power. Sometimes we had people to stay and if he was there, they had bad dreams. It wasn't coincidence; if he was away, they slept well enough. It was his presence." She loosened her grip on his hand and he studied her expression with consternation. What had occurred to him as a whim was confirmed. Her head was raised; there was no mistaking the cold pride in her expression. The sympathy he had felt for her was gone. She was proud of her father. A cold shiver ran down his spine.

He stood still in the dark alley, straining his ears for the sound of the chimes. A gentle breeze stirred against his face, gusting eerily and aimlessly from nowhere to nowhere. In his fancy it was the wind of the moon, and with the stirring of the wind came a dissonant cascade of chimes – not the tune he was expecting; another that he had heard before in a nearby garden caused by a hanging circle of metal pipes with a clanger in the middle which struck the pipes at random when agitated by the wind. For a moment he wondered if this sound had deceived him, had become confused in his mind with that other music. But as he headed back, he felt again the certainty of her presence – she had returned.

He paced his sitting room. He felt unsettled but his fear

for the disturbance of his peace of mind was replaced by excitement. He poured a glass of vodka and paced the room. She had returned. The vodka and the anticipation raised him to a higher state of consciousness. How would she make her presence known? She would not show herself – not yet. He felt the concentration of her mind bent towards him, somewhere out there in the darkness. She would not have changed in that way. The games she played that he had so dreaded, he now awaited eagerly. He was aware of the dreadful torpor that had been his life since she had gone. To rejoin her tantalising dance would be to live again.

He refilled his glass and took a long draught. The tension built up; he felt a pressure in his head and a thrill of excitement so intense it was almost a pain. He felt the pulsing of his blood drumming in his ears. It took a moment to recognise another sound: the ringing of the telephone. A slow smile spread across his face. So that was how it was to be. Who else would call him in the dead of night? His hand shook uncontrollably as he reached for the receiver. There was a bleep, a buzz, silence – and then the first of the chimes, the start of the tune from her locket, followed by a click as the receiver at the other end was replaced.

He held the hand-piece to his ear long after the line had gone dead. He breathed heavily, rejoicing in his heart. She was back. Now he paced the room with a renewed fervour. Her game with him, paused for so many years, was restarted.

It was a change in her behaviour that alerted him. He lay awake in the early hours studying her naked form, stretched out at his side, with a pain in his heart that had permeated his every troubled dream. He was losing her. He faced the agony of this thought with a momentary relief from the ache of uncertainty. It was to replace one dull pain with another much sharper.

Her back was turned against him. She had rolled over in her sleep, trapping her long hair beneath her cheek, pulling it tightly back from her exposed ear and neck, giving an expression of annoyance as if she had swept her hair to one side with an impatient hand. Her knees were drawn up, flattening her long flanks but curiously adding to the impression of her height. One breast hung against the other, stretched out of shape by her position. Her fists were tightly closed with the stress of her dreams; her lower jaw worked, clenching her teeth as if in protest. He drew away from her as if to test the notion that troubled him. He willed her to sense his movement away from her and reach out for him in her sleep, but her mouth worked on; she was lost in her dreams. With a forlorn dread of her remoteness he capitulated to his fear and lay against her, his mouth against her neck, his arms drawing around her. She murmured and moved restlessly away from him. He turned his face to the pillow.

When awake, her eyes avoided his. Driven against every sense he tested her by holding her against him and despaired at the tension of her body that denied his embrace. He turned his face to hers. Her eyes apologised. She smiled weakly and deceitfully. He had to turn away.

He knew and yet the knowledge was too painful to accept. After work he stopped in a bar. A tumbler of vodka persuaded him of other possibilities. Perhaps he had been careless in showing his emotions; the appearance of deceit in her expression was calculated; she was punishing him. Perhaps she felt beneath him; certainly there had been a time when she had revealed this; she was withdrawing from him to protect herself from his rejection that she had persuaded herself was inevitable; and after a third drink had softened his heart – she loved him. He would return, draw her to him and she would reassure him of her love, her cheek wet with tears against his.

When he arrived home, his apartment was empty. Panic and fear overtook him throughout the evening. He found a new significance in her weak deceitful smile that morning: this was the farewell she could not bring herself to make. He went from room to room in a trance, touching her possessions, her underclothes – each a precious vouchsafe that she must return. He saw himself, as if outside his body, witnessing the pathetic spectacle of him kneeling by her dressing table. Tears of self-pity ran down his cheeks. He willed her to return and find him like this. Surely this would soften her heart and make her show mercy to him. But with a chill to his heart, he doubted this thought. What mercy had she shown Boris when she had finished with him? She had found his love troublesome and it had aroused only her contempt. He was suddenly astounded by his blindness. How he had pitied Boris with the smug superiority of an accepted lover; how he had failed to suspect even the possibility that his turn would come. His imagination created an image of her frenzied dance at the dance hall, her body snaking in a shifting pattern but her dance returning again and again in a flowing rhythm to the same steps. How many had there been before Boris? How many broken hearts still pined for her? The pain of these thoughts was unbearable and he searched for an alternative interpretation, remembering the times when she had clung to him, vulnerable and weak, so that he pitied her and felt protective and paternal towards her. And when she had spoken of her nightmare childhood, she had told him with what he believed to be sincerity that she had never told anyone before.

She did not return that night. Steiner could not sleep. With each hour that passed, so increased his disbelief in the possibility that she could inflict so much pain carelessly; it must be that she was angry and punishing him. This was his only comfort through that long night.

She returned the following evening. Throughout the day his mood had swung erratically. He would stay away from home until she had packed and left; he would be angry with her, slap her hard across the face, tell her that he would not allow this. He would be cold, uncaring, demonstrating how she had destroyed the trust that allowed his intimacy, and how he was gone from her emotionally; she had lost his love for ever.

But when confronted with her presence he could act only

to the dictate of a compulsion that was beyond his control. He held his arms out to her. She approached warily, surprised, sulky, suspicious and, with an expression that he had to check to find if it were imagined – disappointed. She stopped short so that he had to draw her towards him. She responded reluctantly and the torment of her cold embrace decided him independently of his will, forcing an incoherent torrent from him.

"I have to know – whatever you've decided – I have to know. Tell me it's over. I love you, but tell me – I can bear it."

She sat down and lit a cigarette. Her hands shook. He sat next to her. Her eyes avoided his.

"I can't live like this. I thought I could, but I can't go on like this."

Her trembling hand reached out for his and he understood: those few words had released her. He took her hand and felt the pain of her grip as she squeezed unconsciously. He rejoiced. She had panicked. He had not lost her.

"You went with someone else. You wanted me to know; you wanted me to be angry, to finish with you and to release you."

She looked him in the eyes for the first time, and nodded her head slowly. Her eyes were curious.

He laughed, partly from a whimsical appreciation of the humour of the situation and partly out of joy; her hand was in his, her attention was with him, and he felt at this moment completely happy.

Steiner looked down at his hand, aware that he was sitting in the same chair in the same place, and that if time were to slip and jump those years, there would be a slender white hand gripping his. He opened a window and lit a cigarette. It was now the deepest quietest hour of the night. All was still, the only noise a rustle of leaves moved by a light wind high in the trees. A distant owl called a double note in vain, unanswered. Steiner thought of the ringing of the telephone earlier. She too was somewhere out in the darkness calling for him.

This thought remained with him through the day, distracting him from his work. Did he imagine that his colleagues stole strange glances in his direction? He tried to concentrate but his thoughts returned again and again to wondering what her next move would be. He resisted the temptation to visit the staff department. He knew there would be a record of her return, but even to make an enquiry would be to alert her. The thought of this sent a shiver of shame through his body, and, surprised by the force of it, he analysed this feeling as not only shame, but fear: that he would subjugate himself again. He remembered the pitiful creature he had been. He had slowly painfully climbed out of that abyss to become human again. How would it be when he saw her again? Would she still have that power over him? He was not ready yet. The prospect of seeing her again had brought a poignancy and romance to his life that had been dormant for all these years. He had dressed himself with care that morning, bathed, washed his hair, pressed his best suit, considered himself in the mirror, and on his walk to work he had breathed in the smells of the cut grass and some wild flower that he could not identify – an exciting aromatic mixture that he remembered from the past and that he wondered at. Why had he not noticed it in all these years this heady potent fragrance that in his imagination he identified as the sperm of a multitude of bursting blooms? He knew that all this was tied to the knowledge of her presence. He embraced the thought, but the fear was over him again: it was too soon; he was not prepared.

On his way home he took a circuitous route, ending up in the alleys behind his apartment. His breathing was laboured and his pulse pounded with the fear of meeting her. He let himself in, relieved and disappointed. He pressed himself against the door as if it were a barrier between him and some pursuing danger; and to reinforce this feeling his legs felt strangely weak as if he had been running. He lit a cigarette to steady his nerves. The telephone rang. He answered it automatically, unsuspecting. This time he was unprepared for the silence that answered him. Then came the first note, prolonged unnaturally in his mind, followed inexorably by the tune he had preserved so perfectly in memory that he anticipated every note, every rise and fall in exact time; forming an echo that reinforced the harmony so strongly that it appeared to increase in volume. He was unaware of the smile that spread across his face – knowing and yet suspicious as if doubtful of his own senses. The tune reached an unbearable crescendo and he had to replace the receiver. The music rang in his head: an ecstatic rhythm, conjuring a vision of her. She stood in darkness. There was no definition to her surroundings except for a light shining directly in her face, catching the sheen of her hair. She was smiling, beckoning – and yet some instinct repelled him. Some quality of her expression troubled him – the light in her eyes, the twisted smile. And it came to him: she was mad. What sort of behaviour was this: to return after all this time and play these peculiar tricks?

He was suddenly aware of some discomfort and pulled at his shirt, it was clinging to his body, soaked though with sweat. Absent-mindedly he wondered at this: it was unusual for him to sweat. He was so wet that he would have to take a bath.

He undressed while the water ran, debating with himself what he should do. How much more of this could he take? Even if he decided to confront her, how would he find her? He lowered himself into the warm water. Something caught his attention. The shock of it made him drop into the bath with a splash. An old woman's face surveyed him from across the room. She stared at him with a cracked harsh expression and yet vacantly as if unaware of his presence. He stared at her in bewilderment for a long moment before understanding: it was an illusion created by a peculiar arrangement of the folds of a towel on the rail. They dissolved into the inanimate before his eyes. He found that he was shaking – an indication of the fragile state of mind her return had induced. And as he immersed himself, lowering his head below the water, he heard a harsh cackle of laughter. He visualised the re-animation of the old woman from the folds of the towel. She would not be dismissed so easily.

This incident decided him; he would not remain passively awaiting her next move. He could not force her into a confrontation but he did not have to stay at her call.

He approached the staff department the next day. With his seniority, his age and the non-specific nature of his work, it was a mere formality to obtain an exit visa, and although the short notice caused the official some consternation, he attended to Steiner's request efficiently and deferentially. Steiner had decided on a trip to West Germany; here he could be sure she could not follow.

He booked into the Interhotel in Magdeburg that night, partly to be ready to catch an early train, but more importantly to avoid another night waiting for the phone call that he knew would come in the night. He thought of the instrument ringing unanswered. Her game would be thwarted for the moment. What would she do? He was certain that his silence would provoke her into action. She would attempt to force an encounter, in the street, at work – but he would not be there. This thought gave him an intense pleasure: he had broken her mastery of him for now.

He settled in the hotel bar, his mind occupied pleasurably with the vision of her frustration. His mood, bolstered by a glass of vodka, was defiant. His awakened memories had revived a long forgotten anger. He knew that he was only postponing the inevitable meeting. He was torn between the desire to see her again and a new fear: that he had been preserved in her memory unchanged, that she would see him as he was now and the attraction she had once felt for him would be gone, whereas he did not doubt that her beauty was undiminished. Perhaps even she deliberately sought him out because of this; perhaps she could not settle with some other for the memory of him that tormented her. An inner voice reasoned with him that it would be a kindness to grant her this peace, if that was her motive; but another voice, venomous with pride, was less compassionate; he must reject her, mortify his love for her, and return the torment she had meted out so mercilessly to him.

They had lived together under a peculiar dynamic, dictated by her wildly fluctuating emotions, and, as if living within some livid dream, he accepted the mad rationale of it as normal.

One morning he arose to find her at breakfast. She was in a foul temper. She hated the inflexible routine of her working life. Steiner knew that by choice she would lie in bed half the morning, or dance or drink, as the mood took her. But he knew too that she was determined to appear professional, in appearance, manner and time keeping, as if a single slip would bring her downfall.

She glanced at him briefly and coldly and the impression of her hostility towards him was so strong that he half expected her to be gone when he arrived home that evening. But to his surprise, he found her waiting for him with an opened bottle of wine. She poured him a glass. She paced the room restlessly. She spoke of her work with agitation. A new head had been posted to her department. Steiner listened in ecstasy; she had been waiting for him. The animation in her face showed that she was relieved to see him. She needed him. He had to make an effort to disguise his pleasure and concentrate on her words. She sat beside him, her face turned to his, searching his eyes, and his heart jumped at the recognition of her peculiar form of seduction: involving him in her affairs. He was unsure if the crisis were real; her work relationships were always fraught. She talked on. She had often spoken of the old department head and of her conviction that he did not like her. She had tried to impress him with her dedication. Steiner had heard her speak many times of this relationship and had come to the private conclusion that it varied with the erratic rhythm of her insecurity, and that it survived because of a sexual attraction that he suspected existed towards her. But the new head was a woman and although few words had been spoken, Sabine sensed an instant hostility.

His concentration wandered as he listened. He did not doubt her intuition, but he guessed at the cold hauteur that had inspired this hostility, and the curious smirk of satisfaction on her face with which she had received the reaction that she had so surely created.

Her hand was in his, and he felt that powerful desire to protect, so much stronger than sexual desire. He felt foolish; he knew her now, knew how he was being manipulated, but was not strong enough to prevent his hand clasping hers. Her sensual smile into his eyes overwhelmed him, but he knew too that she was not innocent of the knowledge of how she affected him.

He made an effort to concentrate on her problem and struggled with the conflicting demands of tact and honesty; it was difficult to find words to suggest that she should modify such an integral part of her personality. She understood his dilemma instantly.

"You think I antagonise her on purpose?"

Steiner abandoned any thought of tact. "Yes – you can be relied on to do that – it's how you protect yourself."

She laughed. "You sound like Hirsch." She squeezed his hand. "You always understand me. I like that. Sometimes though it makes me feel..."

"Exposed?"

She nodded and met his eyes directly. "How is it that you know me so well?"

He shook his head and swallowed a mouthful of wine. "I don't – I don't understand for example how it is that this morning I sensed that I was nothing more to you than a tiresome piece of clothing that was no longer in fashion and needed to be discarded before anyone noticed that you were still wearing it."

"And now?"

"And now..." He could not meet her eyes. He spoke gruffly. *"It all seems right."*

She traced circles with her fingers in his hand. Her voice was low and sincere. "You must be patient." She sighed. "Do you think we'll be like this when we're old, sitting close together holding hands?" She drained her glass. Steiner was still struggling with this amazing question when she jumped up suddenly. "Let's go dancing."

He stared at her, his mind in turmoil. The unnatural pace of her emotions never failed to stun him. The apparently thoughtful question she had just asked – and required no answer to – would occupy him for days, and yet she had left it in a second. His heart sank at this thought, and yet he could not deny her. They had not danced together for a long time. He was flattered that she wanted to go with him. In spite of all his doubts he felt compelled to go along with her mood; to do otherwise would be to torment himself with what might have been. He allowed himself to be led across the complex in a state of ecstasy that came from a perfect summer evening and her hand in his; he let go of it to walk in file down a narrow alley, and when she reached out towards him as they emerged into a precinct, he was pathetically relieved. It took him a moment to identify the surge of emotions that almost unmanned him: warmth for the childlike determination with which she sought his hand, but overwhelming this, fear at his love for her, exposed by the desolation he had felt in those few moments when they had walked in separation. He wondered if she knew the terrible power she had over him. He turned cold at the thought that she might not have taken his hand again in hers.

They reached the dance hall. The music was deafening. He glanced sideways at her; her eyes were bright, her hips writhed to the music. He moved to a table that served as a bar. She disengaged her hand from his but her body pressed against him. Her mouth was against his ear, caressing him as she asked him to order a bottle of wine.

They sat at a side-table. Her attention was taken by the

music and by the people dancing and standing nearby. She smiled at him but he guessed that this was an attempt to reassure him; it must be that his expression revealed the desperation of his thoughts: she wanted to dance rather than to be with him. She could have spent the evening sitting with him, holding hands, talking, making love; she knew that that was what he wanted, but she was restless, she wanted to dance – his presence was incidental.

The music increased in tempo and he could see it pulling at her. She got to her feet, smiling at him briefly before moving to the dance floor. He emptied his glass and refilled it. He tried to interpret her smile and decided that it was from obligation rather than an invitation for him to join her.

He watched her surreptitiously. Her movements were measured; she had not yet lost herself in the music. She was, as usual, surrounded by an entourage of young men dancing close to her.

He ordered another bottle of wine. He was tempted to join her but felt awkward; he needed the wine for courage. It went to his head. He lost the inhibitions that trapped him motionlessly at the dark side-table. But when he got to his feet, his movements were drunken and uncertain. He stood awkwardly on the edge of the dance floor. The music was turned up, the dancers erupted, and he found himself moving uncertainly to the rhythm.

There was a heaving mass of dancers between him and Sabine. He threaded his way through them slowly, and moved back again as he caught a glimpse of her through the throng, recoiling against the feeling that he was spying on her. This added to his awkwardness. He caught sight of himself in a mirror and was horrified at the shrunken shuffling figure that peered back at him. And in contrast, behind him, magnified by the perspective, he caught sight of her – towering, snaking, and moving in perfect time, surrounded by a troupe of dancers who revolved around her like planets in orbit around the sun. She was lost in the music, oblivious to all around her. It seemed as if she was dancing with a lover. Her eyes, focussed into space, caressed with that curious hauteur that excluded all but the one before her. They were one – moving in rhythm, the centre of all attention.

He searched the dancers around her for the one whom she had chosen, but suddenly he understood: she danced with Maria. He was relieved that there was no lover to usurp him, but jealous of this imaginary partner who excluded him with a more certain finality.

He left the dance floor and retreated into the shadows, nursing his torment; they had held hands, they were together, nothing had happened – no argument, no change. He could go to her now, dance with her, hold her, slip his hand into hers, smile and ask if she was enjoying herself; and she would squeeze his hand and return his smile. And yet he sensed the alteration in her mood: she was apart from him now. He challenged this thought defiantly, and arose unsteadily to enact the test demanded by the stupidity of his drunken state. He moved to the dance floor. The music had intensified. He was now so drunk that either by self-deception or loss of inhibition he felt at one with the music. He would dance with her; she would be proud to dance with him, he would replace Maria, people would make space around them, the men giving way enviously before him.

He moved forward unsteadily, his drunken hands reaching out unseeingly towards her; they rested on her swaying hips.

And then came that terrible moment of shame, imprinted in horrible detail on his memory, fixed by the words and melody of the song that beat out across the dance floor – every word and note thundering out accusingly, night after night in livid dreams that re-enacted that dreadful moment... She brushed his hands away. There was a flash of anger in her eyes that he had never seen before. "No, Franz. I don't want us to be seen together."

He was not even aware of backing away. It seemed that the dancers, with Sabine in their centre, recoiled slowly from him until he was returned to the shadows, contracted, shaking, crushed. He wanted to get out of the place that was suddenly so hateful to him. He imagined that the dancers watched him with laughter and contempt. But his legs would not carry him, and he sank into a chair. The music crashed in his ears. A refrain accused, formed from the bass note: "No, Franz, no, no." He drank from the bottle of wine, his eyes drawn against his will across the dance floor to where she danced. It seemed that this act of cruelty had succoured her; her dance was heightened, her arms weaved, her hips swayed – she was magnificent.

He drained the bottle and laughed out aloud at this absurdity; she had crushed him, kicked him in the face as if he was some small pathetic creature that fawned upon her – and what did he do? Admire her – love her – think her magnificent!

He was unaware of the passage of time. He was hopelessly drunk. The music thundered in his head like the crash of breaking waves driven by a storm. He could not look at the dance floor. He was detached from her. Perhaps she had left. He was surprised to look up and find her standing in front of him. He could not read her expression in the darkness. Her voice was even. "Ready?" He got clumsily to his feet. Outside, the night air increased his unsteadiness and he reached for her hand as a child for its mother's. It was only when he felt the warmth of her hand in his that he was aware of his action. It seemed that she took his hand with an initial reluctance followed by acceptance, as if coerced into obeying his wishes.

They walked in silence. He stole a sidelong glance at her. The mood of the dance had passed; she was quiet, reflective, burnt out.

He expected that she would go straight to bed, and was surprised when instead she chose to sit in a chair opposite him. He saw that she watched him. He could not read her mood; she had chosen not to sit next to him, so the intimacy of the early evening had passed, but so too had the moment of anger she had shown on the dance floor. What struck him as curious – he noticed only when she lit a cigarette and her face was half-lit by the orange glow – was that she sat in darkness; he had never known her to do this before.

She began to speak with introversion, talking about herself as if in answer to a question. She spoke of her early childhood; of her grandmother and the children she had played with. Steiner listened with curiosity. This was a new mood, stripped of affectation and intent. She seemed so lost in reminiscence that he wondered if she was even aware of his presence. And as if in reply to this unspoken question, he saw in the half-darkness that her face turned towards him, and though it was too dark to read her expression, the attitude of her head, leaning towards him, told him that she measured his reaction to her words.

She talked on, deep into the night. Steiner found himself listening in a state of semi-consciousness, on the edge of sleep. He formed images from her words that strayed into dreams, entwined with the fantastic. Her voice was changed – clearer and yet more detached. The darkness around her seemed more intense, broken only by the gleaming ember of her cigarette.

"My earliest memory, before I could walk – it must have been because I was in a push-chair – somehow I must have fallen out of it – I suppose I must have hurt myself because I was screaming – but in my memory, I see myself as if I am someone else looking down on this little girl screaming on the ground – but I'm screaming in silence – it must be too distant in time to remember the sounds. But I remember a face coming towards me – I remember the anguish and concern in that face – not my mother but my father – my father loved me." She drew on her cigarette and the glow lit her face. Her eyes were focussed away from him and the orange dot shook from her unseen, unsteady hand. Her voice was distant. "I told you about my father – the bedtime stories – but I missed one detail – I'm sure you guessed – how my father loved me?"

Steiner shook his head. He understood; perhaps subconsciously he had known because he felt no shock. But he continued shaking his head at the dreadful meaning of her words. He sensed that she studied him.

"You surprise me – you know so much – I thought you knew that."

"No – I've never encountered what you speak of."

She mocked: "There is a name for what I speak of but it's not a nice name – not spoken of amongst your nice friends - Schellenberg, Hirsch and the like. And of course such things don't happen to nice little girls. Nice little girls are innocent – they cannot be corrupted – they must themselves be corrupt. And people knew. At the time I felt ashamed that I embarrassed and tainted them. Now I get angry when I think how they knew and did nothing – that was their corruption, not mine. Even my grandmother who I loved and was kind to me – I remember how she frowned when she looked at me sometimes; I know her thoughts now: what a shame I'd been born a girl – and mine the responsibility for that unspoken shame." She laughed shortly. "I learnt, it's true how to make him be nice to me – more than that: to cuddle me, to love me – I could make him love me."

Steiner saw her outline crouch forward as if in defence. He understood the change of tone in her voice and why she needed the darkness to protect her; this was not a new affectation but the truth; she cowered naked before it. He felt a shiver run down his spine and the most urgent desire to go to her and protect her with his arms around her. The emotion he had known as love was nothing to what he felt for her at this moment. But he knew that he must remain motionless, as a hunter watching some shy night creature emerge from its burrow. He watched her light another cigarette with unsteady hands. He willed her to continue; afraid to break this special intimacy, afraid that this moment would be lost forever. He imagined himself leaving her in the chair, going to bed alone, and awaking to find her cold, regretful of this intimacy, and lost from him.

"He was not my blood father, nor she my real mother. I was adopted – one of the thousands fathered by the invading

Russian armies and abandoned after birth by their mothers who could not bear to see those Mongol eyes again; that much at least I know although you would think it was my stepmother who had suffered that disgrace from the flood of tears that flowed before I could get that little bit of knowledge from her. I remember how I despised those tears – the sensibilities of a good communist woman that I dared to disregard by my selfish demand to know who I was – and so much more important to her than the fact that I lived all those years – thirteen to be precise – being lied to every day. I told you the story of my grandmother's locket. She was no more my grandmother than this is her locket." A flash of reflected silver penetrated the darkness. *"In the way of children, I used to pretend that this had truly belonged to the grandmother I had never known. The perversity is that my consolation against that frightful inheritance was the knowledge that I was different, and yet I came to imitate the very cruelty that I considered impossible in me. I became a tormentor just as he. I reached an age when I attained a certain power over men. I used it. I slept with men of all ages. I won't tell you how young I was. I seduced them all; I despised them all. Once I'd had them, it amused me to deny them. Once was usually enough – just occasionally more."*

Steiner interrupted: "And with Boris – and then me?"

Her face turned to him in the darkness. "I never intended that with you."

"And Boris?"

"I came to despise him it is true, but I am talking of the past. I've outgrown all that. Don't misunderstand me, I have no conscience about what I did – except once; there is one I regret, for him and for me – for him because he was only a boy of my age and not right in the head. I tormented him like a cat plays with a half-dead bird. He loved me; that was a special excitement, to examine that in morbid detail. One day he tried to take his life. I had a feeling of exultation that he could have felt that much for me; it was the ultimate compliment. But he was the one amongst them all who did not

deserve what I did to him, and yet he was the one I tormented with special cruelty. It was then that I realised that I was repeating the behaviour of my father, without the excuse of any blood connection. That was what made me leave that poor boy alone."

She talked on, her tone low flat and mesmeric. Steiner's awareness of the present was distorted by the nightmare quality of her words. The room seemed some dark unfamiliar place and Sabine, rocking in her chair as she smoked and talked, was similarly affected in his mind: as if someone he had thought he had known, but was now a stranger. But darker still was the dreamland that stalked him and he was afraid to enter into. Several times he jerked back to consciousness as if wrenching himself from unseen hands that pulled at him. And in this dream-like state he became aware that his surroundings had changed again. Her chair rocked back empty, but as it rocked forward he saw that this was an illusion; that she was still there; her face turned away from him.

"No one would believe it but in fact she is a virgin. She doesn't approve of what I do; she tells me that I am lacking in self-respect. She doesn't know how much that hurts or she would never say it, because Maria is a kind person. Women trust her, even when their husbands are in love with her; they know they can trust her to rebuff their men – she'll not take advantage. She is flattered and she is gentle with them. All her friends are in love with her – men and women – and children adore her. She puts on an act when adults are around, but when she's alone with them, she enters into their world. She understands them in a way others of her age cannot, because she is herself a child – she's never grown up. It sounds like a meaningless remark that people make, but it is truly one of her peculiarities: mentally she hasn't aged; she's still a child." She turned towards Steiner. Some other sense than sight, in the darkness, made him aware of her agitation.

"You'll never come between us."

He was suddenly wide-awake, startled by this inappropriate accusation. He saw a glint of reflected light in the darkness and a moment later heard the chiming tune of her locket, unnaturally loud in the stillness of the night. He was strangely affected, feeling a sudden fatalism and loss as if she were walking away from him to some place where he could not follow. And as if to justify this feeling, she drew herself upright in her chair and her voice was melodic clear and mocking.

"I know that you'll always think of me when you hear this tune." She arose from her chair. Her face, turned towards him briefly, was a pale moon in the first grey of dawn. Her figure cast a shadow up to the ceiling. He could not define the moment of her leaving, as if a mist had drifted through the door.

He sat for a while, alone; afraid to go to bed, afraid of the certainty within him that all was finally over between them. He sought for some consolation in her words that would deny this intuition, but in doing so discovered only confirmation. He felt that for the first time he had met the real Sabine; that some glass protection around her had become displaced and a real conversation had taken place – genuine, sincere and artless. And her naked character was as different as her naked conversation. Underneath the effervescent, flirtatious, excitable, agitated and manipulative exterior was a quiet, introverted, perceptive, sad and highly intelligent creature, whom he had only glimpsed before peering out of her glass window, but who he had now seen naked. He felt certain that this was as forbidden and impossible as to stare at Medusa, but that she rather than he would be turned to stone; that this would be their last time together.

The first bird songs aroused him from his thoughts and he arose from his chair to go to bed.

Steiner finished his drink and ordered another. The hotel bar was almost deserted. Two couples sat at tables. A man sat at the far end of the bar. Steiner glanced at his face in profile. It was a long pointed face with a strong jaw, and framed with black hair showing the first traces of grey. Steiner's casual observation of the man intensified. There was something about the face that attracted and yet at the same time repelled. As the man turned towards him, Steiner observed his features. The cheeks hung heavily and loosely giving a gravity and sadness to the man's expression. The eyes were curiously dark but not cold; they were youthful and held a look of mild surprise as if they had caught sight of the middle-aged body surrounding them and had been caught unawares by the unexpected age of it. Steiner could find nothing sinister in the face and yet felt some vague oppression that he struggled to identify; it was as if the man was familiar; had existed in the past as a stern schoolmaster or commissar – was someone who had held power over him. Steiner concentrated but could not remember such a person; in fact he was certain that this was only an impression rather than a real connection.

The man turned towards Steiner, glancing at him incuriously. Steiner turned away. He felt surprisingly light-headed, as if he had been drinking vodka all night. He counted: the half-empty tumbler in his hand was his third. He looked away from the glass. He felt a sudden strange sensation: he was being watched with an unpleasant oppressive hostility. He glanced sideways. The man's face was in the periphery of his vision. Steiner whipped his head around to face the man, disbelieving, checking that he had not imagined the shocking sight that he had glimpsed: that face in a horrible contorted grimace full of hatred and malevolence such as Steiner had never witnessed before, like some devilish imp captured in a stone gargoyle.

Steiner watched transfixed, too shocked to turn away, even though that evil face threatened him with a dreadful peril. And, as he watched, the features melted back into normal expression. The eyes looked away with the same surprise Steiner had observed before. He was shaken. He drained his glass in one gulp and ordered another, both relieved and surprised that the barman behaved normally. This must have been some secret expression that he had witnessed by accident, not, as he had supposed, directed at him. But he was shaken. Surely the man must be a madman who could turn at any moment. Steiner felt uncomfortable. He finished his drink and went to his room. He sat on the bed. His legs felt unsteady. He lit a cigarette.

The first rays of sunshine dispelled the greyness of the room and cast across Steiner's bed. His dreams held more fear for him than reality and he dressed quickly. He must see her to settle this uncertainty. He heard her moving quietly about. He came face to face with her as he left his room; he paused to let her pass; one look at her face justified all his fears: she directed a cold glance at him before passing in silence.

He returned to his room. He would wait for her to go. Tears of self-pity ran down his cheeks. He could not face her.

Throughout the day the memory of her coldness pervaded his every thought. His self-pity turned to anger. He surprised himself by the novelty and force of this new mood; he was not easily angered. He turned over in his mind all that had happened, feeling the anger flare again at the memory of her rebuff on the dance-floor: she had shamed him – and now she rejected him in his own home. In spite of his anger, he recognised the hurt to his pride. He had never thought of himself as proud but she had found this weakness. He resolved to hide this from her, to feign indifference and deny her the knowledge of how severely she had wounded him. But perversely, the very thought of trying to suppress his anger only aroused him further. Rejection, shame, humiliation – the words echoed in his head, demanding and accusing. He would throw her out. She had rejected him – then she must go. It was his turn to reject. He would never see her again. This thought would not be passed over. He examined it repeatedly and obsessively; it appalled and fascinated him. His heart pleaded with him but he had found a new grim resolve. This he knew was right; this must be done to be strong and regain control over his life. He knew that he would punish himself out of all proportion to any minor irritation or inconvenience he would cause her – but he would do it and put an end to his hurt; she would shame him no more. His only doubt concerned practicalities. It would take her time to be re-allocated a new apartment. He panicked at the thought of this delay, of further nights at home with her. He could not face this; he must go himself and stay in Magdeburg or put up with friends until she had gone.

He left work early, confronting her as soon as she returned. His anger disappeared in an instant as if it were an electrical charge that had been grounded. He delivered the words of his speech in sorrow. He would leave that evening. He had hoped she would ask where he would go – he had imagined his enjoyment at denying her this information – but she didn't ask. Her reaction surprised him. She replied in a stilted artificial voice, professing sorrow for the hurt she had caused him. He wondered if she were sincere; she sounded genuine, and in spite of the artificial quality of her voice, she did not display the hauteur and triumphalism that he had expected.

He had been unable to look at her, but now that all was said, he observed her for the first time. She stared directly and curiously into his eyes. He saw that she was surprised. He turned away, overtaken by all the emotions that had been suspended by the anxiety of this confrontation. Now he understood the meaning of what he had done. Now he was committed to never seeing her again, and the hope that he had not admitted to was dashed: that faced with him leaving, she would soften towards him and not let him go. But her reply had been firm and defiant. She had understood his challenge and accepted it. He watched her move across the room. Now finally he had lost her. He loved her more than ever and dreaded living without her. His future without her would be empty and meaningless. His resolve now was driven by pride alone.

She stood in the corner of the room, bent over her record player, one of the few possessions she had brought with her. It was old and poor quality, but it was precious to her. This was one of her quirks that Steiner loved her for. Now, as he watched her, the pathos was unbearable.

Her movements were unnatural. His heart leapt – she was upset. Her long neck was exposed as she bent over the player. Her hair fell forward, covering her face. She appeared to concentrate on her movements as if there were some grave purpose to each action.

The music played. Steiner was startled. He had never heard her play this type of music. He had not heard the like of it since his mother had played it when he was a young child – dissonant harsh, tinny instruments and a cracked cheap lyric, conjuring up images of a time long past: horse carriages drawn up outside a chateau, flimsily-dressed dancers drinking champagne, forming perilous liaisons, dancing in decadence and depravity into the night. He found the music strangely appropriate. In his imagination, the shadowy long-dead figures gained definition. They danced on a lawn illuminated by a bright silver moon. One figure stood out from the others. She was taller and her dancing more abandoned. Her hair was held back by a black velvet band. She wore a silver locket around her neck. Her features were familiar, passed back through the influence of the silver trinket around her neck rather than ties of blood.

Steiner turned his back on this absurd fancy. He packed a case rapidly. Every minute's delay was unbearable now. He checked the case before closing it. The thought of having to return while she was still there sent him into a spasm of anxiety. He stood for a moment looking around the room. The music from below repeated and increased in volume. He descended the stairs slowly and paused at the doorway. She faced away from him, bent over the record player, playing one short piece, repeating it, and then moving to another. There was something peculiarly obsessive about the sight of her bent neck and working hands. He moved away, closed the door on that strange oblivious figure. Tears poured down his cheeks.

Steiner walked down the platform until he found an almost empty carriage. He settled himself into a seat facing the engine and moments later the train started off with a silent jolt. Within minutes the dark forbidding town of dirty stone buildings was left behind. He settled back with the window open, breathing in the fresh smell of countryside.

Every step took him away from her and could not be retraced; every step took him into a new and empty life. He paused, not looking back but listening for the sound of running steps. He imagined them in the silence; heard them approach, imagined her tears and the surrender in her voice as she begged him to return and mend this foolish quarrel – but all was silent.

He had approached Schellenberg earlier in the day. His friend had not only been delighted at the prospect of Steiner staying for some time, insisting he should stay as long as he wished, but was also surprisingly sympathetic. Steiner had often wondered if Schellenberg was fully aware of anything that went on outside his science, and was humbled by his friend's concern, which was earnest and lacking in the vagueness without which Schellenberg was almost unrecognisable. He patted Steiner gently on the back. "Woman trouble." He nodded knowingly, and Steiner was so amazed by the discernment and sympathy in his expression that he was rescued by involuntary laughter from an intense and sentimental gratitude that threatened to express itself in tears.

Now, as Steiner turned towards the Schellenbergs' apartment block, he was apprehensive of imposing on them. They were good friends but they had their own life and their own sadness. But Sylvie answered the door, and his uncertainties, with a hug that was so warm and maternal that this time there was no holding back his tears.

When the Schellenbergs had sat him down and fetched him a drink, they would not allow any commonplace conversation; Sylvie insisted that he told the whole story. In spite of his misery, Steiner smiled inwardly at the complicity behind this scene: Schellenberg extracted from his work, sitting next to his wife, holding her hand and nodding in agreement as she urged Steiner to talk – she being the leader in this, with a woman's knowledge of what was best.

And it was a relief to tell them – every detail of his affair, from the first meeting up until this final parting. He was aware, as he spoke, of the keen concentration of Sylvie, and recognised his own motive in the telling of the story. He clung to the pathetic hope that Sylvie would interpret Sabine's behaviour in such a way as to conclude that she loved him and would return to him. And even as he told the story, it seemed to him that there were so many indications of her love for him, that it was truly only a quarrel that would soon be mended. Such was his assurance that he felt a momentary irritation at the sight of Sylvie's grave expression, and had to resist an hysterical impulse to tell her not to be so serious, no one had died, and it was not so uncommon for couples to argue.

But this moment was soon overtaken by curiosity. Sylvie was a perceptive woman. He needed to ask her a question that had been on his mind for a long time, even though he was fearful of her reply.

"Do you remember when you met her? You looked at me just as you were leaving, and you shook your head at me."

Sylvie glanced at her husband and pursed her lips as if in defiance of his unspoken censure.

"We are old friends, Franz. We are both very fond of you, too fond for anything but straight talking. I will tell you, if that is what you want."

Steiner nodded.

"The answer to your question is that although I did not disapprove of her, I disapproved of you and her as a couple. You had talked of her for a long time – when she was with

Boris. You perhaps weren't aware of how much you talked of her. Anyone who knew you could see what was happening," she glanced at her husband, *"even Schellenberg. This girl, supposedly your friend's lover, had designs on you. It amused me at the time. I felt no need to alert you to another woman's guile. How often it happens that a man believes himself to have approached a woman when she, for a long time, has positioned events to make it so."* Sylvie squeezed her husband's hand and darted him a pointed look. Schellenberg raised his eyebrows comically at Steiner and they all laughed. Sylvie continued: *"There was one aspect to it though that I didn't like – just as it was obvious that you were falling in love with her, it was also obvious how besotted poor Boris was – and he, so guileless but so passionate – it's wrong with a man like that. Still – I hadn't met her, I only knew what I had heard. I reserved judgement."*

"You always do – that's why I was so surprised by your reaction to her."

"And then I met her – and I recognised her." Sylvie hurried to answer the look of surprise on Steiner's face. *"No – not what you think – I'd never physically met her. I mean recognise in another sense: I knew who she was and what she was. I could see all that you liked in her: sensitive, beautiful, bright – perhaps more so than even she knows herself – but above all, vulnerable, and I could see the return side of that: how protective you felt towards her, how desperate you were for us all to like her…"*

Schellenberg, attempting to follow all this without letting his mind wander back to his experiments, perked up suddenly as if he felt the need to prove that he was paying attention.

"That's very well put, my dear – the return side – the positive output from the anode and the return to the cathode."

Sylvie turned to her husband with a frown, wondering, as she so often wondered, at the peculiar dysfunction of Schellenburg's thought process on any subject other than science, saw to her amazement that this was a well-intentioned and supposedly serious remark, blinked her eyes briefly as if to wipe away this absurdity, and continued:

"I wanted to like her for your sake, but the one quality, so striking that it surpassed all others, you had omitted to mention... how terribly unstable she is."

Steiner nodded thoughtfully. "I've known that for some time now – but I don't understand how you could – at least not from that one meeting. I remember that evening. I remember how relieved I was that it went so well, and yet you must have picked up on something.

"She was detached, talking to us and listening to us, but far removed from us as if the other side of a barrier: one that was constructed by her for her own protection. She needed to be remote and not to belong to us, so that she could watch us from afar with a distant smile and not be in danger from any false enticement that our friendly overtures might deceive her into.

"There is a kind of game she plays when she's not at ease. She has a friend, Maria – a girlfriend who has a great influence on her – so much so that I think now Sabine is afraid of Maria's dominance and is trying to break it. She has, without doubt, deliberately ensured that I never meet her. But there is no match for Maria; she is wittier, sharper, more beautiful and, what I find strange, more moral than anyone else in the world. And all are so diminished by Maria's presence, that when Sabine feels the need, she conjures up an image of Maria and converses secretly with her, so that she has no need to feel awed by any other's presence."

Schellenberg stared and shook his head. He had been struggling manfully to keep up with the conversation, but the concept of people inventing imaginary friends to talk to was incomprehensible to him. Sylvie, however, nodded as if none of this was unexpected to her.

"She was laughing at us, mocking us – all of us – even you, Franz – not overtly but with a smirk, apparently when she thought she was unobserved but when I suspect she knew she was."

"That's exactly it. Our conversation and everything about us was made so small and trivial by the presence of Maria."

Sylvie looked unconvinced. "Maria is only the instrument. The contempt is hers. This may be painful to you unless you already know: Did you see what she was doing to Hirsch?" Steiner shook his head. "Touching him under the table."

Steiner was distracted from his amazement by the sight of Schellenberg, who was now so completely bewildered that he sat rigidly with his eyes tightly closed, clutching at his cheeks with his hands, as if grappling with some impossible equation.

Sylvie continued: "You know how he makes a fool of himself with women. I've often told Ulrika to take no notice; he can't help himself, and it never leads to anything. As for Sabine, she had no interest in him other than to amuse herself with the power she had over him, one of the leading scientists in the laboratories. It was a pretty game – that's why I say I recognised her: I recognised that behaviour."

Steiner considered. "It does fit a certain pattern. I have some understanding of her. Maybe I flatter myself but I have a feeling that I've been closer to her than most."

"I don't doubt that. In fact that closeness and the feelings she has for you are probably, at this time in her life, quite unbearable to her; they compel her to push you away."

Schellenberg was suddenly enlightened. "Stars do that – at a certain stage." He frowned as if at a sudden doubt. "Don't know if it's helpful at all, but that's what they do – the gravity attracts, pulls everything in until the matter is super-compressed, until a certain density is reached, and then the whole lot explodes."

Sylvie looked at her husband cryptically. "A certain density, you say." She smiled suddenly. "It is helpful, Schellenberg – it is exactly as you say."

Sylvie caught Steiner's eye and they both erupted with laughter. Schellenberg beamed. He occasionally made people laugh and he was never quite sure how. It seemed to him that other people were made differently to him: they had a whimsical and erratic humour that was triggered almost randomly, just as a build up of static electricity in the clouds would discharge to a point on the ground. You could not predict how or exactly why this point was chosen. The thunder of their laughter was equally capricious but he was delighted to have been the cause of it.

Steiner turned to Sylvie. "What did you mean by: 'at this time of her life'?"

"I can see what there is between you: that chemistry that makes you attractive to each other. I suppose what I meant is that she might learn to cope with that in the future."

"Is that it – she can't cope?" Steiner spoke these words with a particular helplessness, convinced of their significance and weighed down by them. He wanted to challenge, question and deny Sylvie's fatalism, but every word she had spoken proved her superior understanding. For a moment again he was angry with her, as if she sat in judgement and condemned him, but this feeling passed in an instant, leaving him ashamed at the unfairness of this thought. But his obsessive persistent hope found a voice.

"I agree with you. You seem to have an extraordinary insight into her nature. But could it work if we spent time apart, and came together again when she is older?"

Sylvie considered. "Possibly, but I doubt it."

"Why?"

"Because of what has happened between you, because she feels out of control of her emotions, and because of the pace of her life. You will become a part of her history; part of a dissonant tune without rhythm where the same notes cannot be played twice."

Schellenberg nodded his head excitedly, tuning in suddenly to this abstract concept, and muttered to himself as if ashamed to pronounce his idea: "Chaos."

They laughed again. Steiner was surprised to be able to laugh, not just to laugh but to feel a surprising elation, as if he had just escaped from some mortal danger and was almost hysterical with joy and relief at being alive. And this peculiar state was intensified by the thought of how dear these best of friends were to him and of how he loved them.

The interminable formalities of crossing the western frontier at Marienborn meant that it was early evening when the train pulled into a country station, apparently in the middle of nowhere. He was relieved to stretch his legs as he stepped onto the platform. A guard stood at an open door at the front of the train, chatting to the unseen driver. Steiner smiled to himself; capitalist Germans seemed little different to communist ones.

Two other passengers alighted: a smartly dressed young woman, and a casually dressed middle-aged man. Both rapidly overtook Steiner's slow amble. The station was at the end of the line. A picturesque navigation canal crossed beyond it.

He paused on an arched stone bridge to watch a barge pass underneath towards a line of similar boats queuing at a lock gate. The sound of distant laughter and conversation from the boats made him feel suddenly lonely. He turned away. The path joined a single-track road, lined by ancient elms on each side.

A stack of chimneys over the tree line announced his destination. He paused as the hotel came into view, breathed in the country air which was invigorating and scented with cowslips and hay.

He was shown to his room by a fat, jovial manager, who praised the good walks, fishing and beautiful countryside. After a bath and a change of clothes he ate a leisurely dinner in the almost empty restaurant, and retired to the bar, which was surprisingly busy. The manager explained that this was a popular stopping place for holidaymakers on the canal. This remark gave Steiner an insight into the atmosphere in the bar. A group of people sat at every table laughing and joking or in animated discussion, but the accents and fashions of each were different; he presumed them to be the inhabitants of boats from different places. This was the opposite extreme from life in the laboratories where everybody knew each other and shared a commonality of dress and conversation.

A man in late middle age, carrying an instrument-case, entered the bar from outside. He looked out of place, dressed in a formal suit that was well worn to the point of shabbiness. He paused for a moment to look around. Without appearing to know anyone his pose was at ease as if this was his home and the clientele his guests.

The manager had a stein of beer ready for him at the bar and the man returned with it to a corner near to Steiner. He unpacked his instrument – an ancient-looking accordion. He plugged in wires to an amplifier, loudspeakers, and a mysterious-looking black box. Steiner was intrigued. He had not encountered an amplified accordion before, and the purpose of the box mystified him; it became clear after the man started to play, it providing a background of other instruments. The man was a master; the first few songs were well-known tunes. Conversation faltered around the bar as people fell silent to listen. The end of each tune was greeted with polite applause. But after a time the tunes became more obscure. The electronic box supplied an increasingly insidious and varied backing, from deep strings, violins and percussion to electronic-sounding bagpipes. And the insistent, commanding accordion led off into wild, complicated melodies that affected Steiner strangely.

The atmosphere of the room changed. The faces around the tables seemed to recede and darken – some, nearby, lost definition, and others, further away, gained sharp focus. One in particular caught Steiner's attention. It was that of a young man who had been laughing with his friends and was now silent. It was a long pale face with thin compressed lips and dark oval eyes. The expression on this face was thin and mean, as if worn to premature age by a hard existence. The eyes, turned to Steiner, were unseeing as if occupied by cares. It was hard to imagine them ever having smiled.

Steiner turned on an impulse to the musician with an absurd suspicion that he was playing some dark game with the clientele. But the man's face was inscrutable. He played now to an enraptured audience, his music uninterrupted by a whisper or even an exchanged glance. All were under his spell. And Steiner suddenly understood the nature of the game he suspected: all who listened were being pulled back in time by this music that had started so innocently but was now wild and primeval. In spite of this, he was unafraid, and offered himself up willingly to this adventure. He didn't want the music to stop; it aroused pleasure and excitement in his heart. He found his attention drawn to one of the curtained windows, willed the curtains to draw back and reveal the darkness beyond. Would it be as he had seen earlier: the tree-lined road to the station? Or would it be as this place had once been centuries before? A moonlit moor perhaps, roamed by bison and wolves, crossed by the ruts of a cart-track leading to a settlement of timber houses lit by the flicker of oil-lamps from within.

The music stopped. The musician reached for his glass of beer to a burst of applause. Conversation restarted. Steiner drank from his glass, returning from the surreal but still elated by the strange and wonderful music. This pleasurable feeling persisted. It was not just the music; he searched for its source – Sabine. Was it pleasure or relief? Relief he decided; he was relaxed now; he was safe here, beyond her siren call. But it was a pleasure too, however unworthy, to think of her repeated phone calls, unanswered. He lit a cigarette, savouring this thought. He imagined her frustration – more than frustration: panic – at her loss of control. And he knew as a certainty what would follow: the impatient pacing up and down, wine, cigarettes, frenzied music; her pace increasing, her beautiful eyes, distant and thoughtful, perturbed but not angry – and then, sudden impatient action which was beyond her command. That was how it would be.

Steiner had been at the Schellenbergs' for a week when the call came. He was waiting for it. That time came with the mysterious rhythm of her mind: the day before the weekend as the light faded. He had rushed home early from his work to be sure of being there, waiting and hoping. Every minute seemed interminably long. His heart leapt at the sound of the telephone; its buzzing pulse caressing, insistent and unanswered. He would not answer it even though he was drawn pathetically by the sound, like an insect to a night flame. He stood over the instrument, watching it; deflated when finally it stopped. He visualised her replacing the receiver, her annoyance and impatience, the hang of her head; and suddenly he was overcome with pity; he wanted to be there to hold her and to comfort her. He stood motionless, watching the telephone, willing it to ring again. The afternoon shadows lengthened through the window, just as Boris had described. There was a noise at the door. His heart leapt again. He knew how she panicked at being ignored. Could it be? Sylvie let herself in and Steiner slipped guiltily away. The telephone rang again.

Sylvie picked up the receiver. "Hello." Steiner heard her mutter something but did not catch her words. She caught sight of Steiner and her frown lifted. "Strange – no one there." She looked at him, and an unspoken understanding passed between them.

Steiner took a sip of beer. The long day had tired him. He looked forward with pleasure to a night's sleep and to lying in late the following morning, followed by a leisurely breakfast. The musician had packed his instrument and left, and there were only two groups left in the bar. Steiner observed them casually, his mind occupied with the question of what she would do when her calls were unanswered. She would try to force a confrontation, and when she found he had gone away, what would she do?

His glance fixed unconsciously on a table across the room. An unpleasant familiarity infiltrated his thoughts as he focussed on a figure facing him across the bar. He knew that face. His hand suddenly dropped onto the table as he lost control of his grip. It was the man in the hotel bar, the one who he had caught for an instant with such a malevolent grimace.

Steiner got up suddenly, not wishing to be recognised. The man must have been on the train. He must have followed him; to have come all this way across the western border and to this remote place could not be a coincidence.

He returned to his room. He did not remember falling asleep but, suddenly conscious, was aware of vague memories of a disturbing dream that still troubled him. All was still. A crescent moon shimmered in the centre of the window. He turned onto his side and closed his eyes, but was almost immediately disturbed by the sound of a loud whispering voice. Steiner sat up suddenly and as he did so a second voice hushed the first with a commanding, "Sh, sh, sh."

Steiner stayed still and listened; all was silent. He began to wonder if he had dropped off to sleep for a moment and had dreamt the voices. The manager had told him that the other rooms were vacant. He lay down again. As his head touched the pillow, the whispering started again, and Steiner jerked upright in bed. The same happened three times, until he jumped out of bed, now angry at this peculiar disturbance to his sleep. His first impulse was to storm into the next room and accost whoever was there, but all was quiet again. He pressed his ear to the connecting wall and listened. He felt foolish standing in a pool of moonlight, half-naked in his nightshirt, with his ear pressed to the wall, but he would not be deceived this time; someone nearby was listening and waiting. And sure enough, starting so softly that Steiner wondered if it were his imagination, came the faintest sound of a single voice, hushed to a surreptitious whisper. Each murmur of sound was followed by a moment of silence as the voice listened intently before restarting.

Steiner was puzzled and angry. Who was this disturbing his sleep? There had been two voices earlier, loud enough to awaken him, yet now there was only one, and so quiet as to be indistinct. He was aware of the lifting of the hairs on the back of his neck at the knowledge that somewhere across the wall they were playing games with him.

As he listened, the speech became more familiar to him, as if at any moment the words would become intelligible. The voice, gaining in definition, was coarse, cracked and harsh.

"Mister fuckin' nosy – you listen, you'll hear all right, but you won't like what you hear – teach you to be so fuckin' nosy."

Steiner shuddered, not just at the words, but at the uncouthness of the voice, and at a deeper subliminal trouble – he knew that voice.

He listened for the reply from the other, but the same voice continued: "Yes, you, Mister fuckin' nosy with your ear pressed to the wall."

Steiner leapt back in fright. The voice had suddenly crossed the wall and was directly in his ear, hissing with venom and malevolence. The voice belonged to the man in the hotel bar, the one who had followed him. He shrank back against the bed. His heartbeat pounded in his ears. All was mercifully silent. He stood up, searching the moonlit room for the owner of the voice, spinning suddenly around in case by some trick the devil was behind him. But the room was empty; the voice had gone.

He breakfasted late as he had promised himself. It was a particular pleasure not to have to rush. The manager served him coffee. He eyed Steiner warily.

"Did you not sleep well?"

Steiner frowned at a vague memory. "Is it so obvious? Do I look tired?

The manager shook his head. "Calling out, you were – shouting out – woke the wife up. She was going to see that you were all right, but I reckon you went back to sleep."

Steiner was embarrassed. "I'm very sorry; I had no idea. It must have been a nightmare. I really am very sorry to have disturbed you."

The manager picked up an empty plate. "Don't worry – we're soon to sleep again, the wife and I."

Steiner was puzzled. He had a vague recollection of an unpleasant dream in the night, but had no memory of calling out. He suspected the manager of exaggeration.

Later in the morning he went for a walk, deciding to explore the canal. The manager had told him of an inn, an hour's walk along the towpath. He relaxed in the late summer sunshine, enjoying the scenery. He remembered his thoughts of the night before, and imagined the gnarled old elms as they must have been as saplings; imagined the scene as it must have been when they were planted, perhaps a hundred years before.

He joined the towpath, passed the moored barges and crossed a high-arched stone bridge into open pastures bisected by the winding canal.

The telephone call came again, one week later, at that special time. This time he was alone. He had been concentrating on this moment all week. His hand hovered above the instrument for a long moment; afraid to pick it up, afraid that it was not her, and afraid that it was.

He heard her sigh, as if with relief, when he answered; and from her first words – the softness, remorse and intimacy – he knew that this dreadful foolish quarrel was over. She asked how he had been; she called him 'Muffelchen' – the pet name that he had never liked, but that now seemed the most precious and endearing of all names. He surprised himself by succeeding in mastering his emotions; he was friendly but casual; he talked of work amusingly and made her laugh, although he detected a note of surprise in her voice – disappointment even; he fancied that he cheated the destructive side of her nature out of its prey. She seemed content to listen to him as if she gained some relief from this conversation. His elation was suddenly dampened by doubt: perhaps she wanted to change the note on which their affair had ended, to normalise relations between them. He knew how much she cared about other people's opinion of her; it would not suit her for others to observe the coldness between them; it would be an embarrassment to her. This doubt was reinforced by her next words: she had found new lodgings, he could move back soon, she would tell him when. He felt the shame of being patronised and ended the conversation abruptly.

Her next call came at the same time the following week. This time he knew that he would not be able to recapture the ease with he had spoken to her before; and this time she too was different: she told him coldly and abruptly that his apartment would be vacant for his return the following Monday. His only consoling thought as he replaced the receiver was that her curtness had sounded forced; behind it he detected hurt.

He made his announcement to the Schellenbergs over dinner. He thanked them for their hospitality and their friendship. Schellenberg appeared moved.

"It's been our pleasure and you must come again soon – stay as long as you like. There's always a bed for you, isn't there, Sylvie?" He turned to his wife and she smiled in agreement.

"Of course. Will you go back straight away?"

Steiner considered. "I might stay on a few days, if you really don't mind."

Sylvie looked at him curiously. "You think she'll stay on after Monday?"

Steiner nodded. "You've only met her the once and yet you seem to understand her so well."

"I'm only agreeing with what you evidently already suspect. That sort of perception is unusual in a man." She sighed. "I'll tell you something you want to hear, even though I wish it was otherwise – you've not heard the last of her."

"You're right. I know she'll still be there if I go back when she says – and I so want to do that."

"Why don't you?

Steiner smiled. "Pride. She will have taken me for a fool.

I'm more afraid of that than not seeing her; I'm afraid of the power she has over me; I'm afraid to come when she beckons."

Sylvie nodded as though this was the reply she had expected. She looked at him directly with her steady grey eyes. "You're certainly not a fool; you understand the tune she would have you dance to – and it's a seductive one."

Steiner waited until the following Tuesday. He could not resist putting his guess to the test. He approached his apartment from the rear alley. A light was on in his bedroom. The curtains were closed. Nothing moved. He stood in the alley watching and waiting. Perhaps she had gone just as she had said, and left a light on. He was on the point of leaving when a shadow passed across the curtains. He moved back into the shadows. The light went out, but a moment later the curtains moved surreptitiously. He stood motionless, seeing her in his mind, probing the darkness for any movement. Then the light went back on, followed a moment later by the heavy bass note of music – her music; and a moving silhouette cast upon the curtains – the lithe snaking dance he knew so well.

He watched for a while before slipping away. There was something eerie and disturbing about that writhing shadow. He felt strong; he had not fallen into her trap – that would have angered her; he was strong and she was weak; not just weak, a little mad. But then he had a vision of her fey smile as she danced, careless of all in her abandonment. He was fooling himself; it was she that had the power over him; she had only to smile, to beckon, and he would be drawn to her as inexorably as the tides to the moon.

Steiner was relieved to see the inn on a bend in the canal before him. He lingered over lunch, enjoying the busy, jolly life of the river, the comings and goings along the towpath between the barges and the inn. There were families of all ages. He noticed, as on the previous night, their disparity of dress, accent and appearance, but these were nullified by the camaraderie of the canal. Children played together, teenagers flirted with determined German earnestness, and adults conversed between the tables. He felt alone; it seemed he was excluded from them all; he alone had some unpermitted trait, some extreme mutation that made him unfit for human intercourse. He would not mind so much if they gave some recognition of this: a guilty avoidance of his eye or a surreptitious awkward glance, but they looked through him and past him, oblivious to any human sensibility that might exist in this excluded creature. To match his mood, the afternoon sky began to darken. He got to his feet, feeling unexpectedly weak.

The journey back seemed long and threatening. He tried to reason with himself against this irrational anxiety: it wasn't such a long walk; he could not get lost, he only had to follow the canal; it didn't matter if it rained, he had a change of clothes back at the hotel. But the weakness in his legs persisted. He was close to panicking. He passed the last of the moored barges, aware that he was scowling at a woman relaxing in a deck-chair; angry with her indifference, holding her responsible for this debilitating sensation that troubled and weakened him.

The clouds darkened ominously as he made his way along the towpath. He reckoned himself to be halfway back when the first heavy drops of rain fell. A sudden gust of wind blew at him as if some invisible giant had pursed his lips and puffed at him with mischievous intent. Steiner lowered his head against the blinding sheet rain. A gale now howled in his ears, whistling and singing. The horizon was lit with a jagged mosaic of lightning that spread across the blackened sky, followed by a rolling thunderclap that shook the ground beneath him. He trudged on, now soaked to the skin. He had never known such a storm. A fizzing crack made him jump; a line of tall conifers was being whipped by the wind against a power line, arcing orange, and spitting.

At last he reached the road, breathing deeply with relief to be in sight of the hotel. A shadow caught his attention – a fellow traveller making his way through the storm; but what a strange character. In the darkness, the figure lacked definition, but there was something inappropriate about his movements. He was a thin dapper looking man, high stepping – almost prancing. Steiner was irritated. What was the meaning of this? Was the impudent fellow mocking his trudging pace with this ridiculous prancing step? But then his irritation turned to a smile as a flash of lightening illuminated the figure – it wasn't a real man; only a funny little black caricature prancing along by the side of the road. Steiner laughed at this absurdity, and was still shaking his head when he reached the hotel.

The manager greeted him at the bar with a sympathetic, almost apologetic, shake of his head.

"Seemed set fine this morning; I would have warned you if I'd thought it was going to turn. We get a few showers around here, particularly at the end of the season."

Steiner laughed. "An end of summer shower was it? Well you can pour me a large one to drink your health and toast your local showers." And after the manager had obliged and Steiner was warmed by two fingers of vodka: "Showers indeed! I've never seen anything like it; the wind whipping the trees into the power lines and setting the tops on fire; lightning like I've never seen before – but the thunder – that was really spectacular."

The manger looked dubious. "Must have been away a bit from here – can't say I heard any thunder."

Steiner finished his drink in one draught and went to get changed. The manager irritated him; his doubtful look was not lost on Steiner; what a peculiar fellow – why should he try to belittle the storm?

He was relieved to get out of his wet clothes and soak in a hot bath. The warmth restored him; it was worth getting cold and wet for this. And in this comfortable state, his mind turned to Sabine. She would be searching for him now, almost certainly checking his apartment at night, only to find it in darkness.

Steiner stood concealed in the back alleys behind his apartment. This was the third night he had returned. Light blazed through the open curtains but there was no sound or movement from within. He lit a cigarette, enjoying the smoke in the night air and intensifying this moment of relief from his misery. There was no reason now to stay; he had found what he needed to know: that she was still there – and yet he stayed, drawn by the knowledge of her nearness. He turned away reluctantly, but his mood persisted; he had thwarted her game; she had tried to lure him into a confrontation; he pictured her annoyance with satisfaction. But then his imagination conjured another scene: she waited for him, alone and vulnerable, needing him, distressed by his absence; and his complacency was replaced by a dreadful sense of loss and yearning.

He repeated his vigil for the next two nights, and on the third, he returned to find his apartment in darkness. He moved along the alley until he stood directly before the darkened window. Now his loss seemed final. He gave way and wept.

He returned the next morning, wanting to get this grim moment over with. Even as he opened the door, he hoped that she would be there. But the apartment was empty and silent. He moved from room to room, every step a painful rediscovery of places that had so recently been homely and familiar but now were desolate. He wondered if he could ever be at peace in this place; wondered if he could ever spend a night here on his own.

He stopped on the threshold of his bedroom door. A pair of shoes – her shoes – stood neatly together in the centre of the floor. He stared at them mesmerised, puzzled, disturbed, but overwhelmingly and irrationally elated. He recognised them as her most expensive and treasured possessions: high-heeled red shiny leather dancing shoes, bought from Italy with American dollars. For a long moment their presence seemed to forbid his entry into the room; they were so intimately hers that they claimed the surroundings as her private domain. Another force compelled him towards them. He circled around them. He was reminded of how once he had seen a fox in the back alleys, and how he had taken pity on the creature and put out a bowl of meat for it; how he had watched it through a crack in the curtains circling round and round before it plucked up the courage to take the food. He understood the creature now – how marvel and fear, when in balance, allowed only movement in a circle. He saw with satisfaction the care with which the shoes had been placed together – the toes and heels in perfect alignment. He saw her bent over them; saw the lines of concentration on her forehead as she made minute adjustments to obtain perfect symmetry. He recognised the nature of his elation: the placing of the shoes was deliberate; if she had left them behind by accident they would be concealed in some place where she had overlooked them, not arranged in the centre of the floor with her obsessive exactness; and she would not leave her favourite shoes behind by accident. The message was cryptic and typical of her; designed to puzzle and to make him think of her; to manipulate, to reserve a claim to this territory: the place where they had made love.

He sat on his bed and lit a cigarette. He considered moving the shoes but could not bring himself to touch them; they represented the thin thread of communication that was all that remained between them now. There would be a telephone call, or she would turn up at his door to claim these shoes that she has accidentally left behind. He imagined that moment and yearned for it, and yet at the same time felt fearful and defiant; he was determined not to be at the mercy of her manipulation.

He prepared for bed, tormented by these opposing emotions. As he pulled back the covers, a scrap of black material caught his eye – a pair of her knickers. His mood changed to anger; there was subtlety, humour, pathos even, in the arrangement of her shoes on the floor, but in this he found only crudeness and cruelty. He picked up the shoes and threw them violently out of the open door and heard them slam up against the opposite wall.

The next day, he hurried home from work, apprehensive and excited at the thought that she would make an attempt to contact him. Sure enough, a note had been posted through his door. It was curt and formal: she 'would be grateful if he would forward any messages and telephone calls'. She gave her address and telephone number, and ended the note simply: 'Sabine'.

He kept a block of paper by the telephone. This was another of his most precious possessions. He had begged it from the yard of a printing works as a child. It was a trimming from an oversize ream of blue writing paper. He remembered how the print worker had been amused by the little boy's gratitude, and gone so far as to gum the sheets for him so that they formed a miniature pad. This pad had followed him through school and university. In those reckless days, he would sometimes use up a sheet in a week. But now, with the conservatism brought by age, he atoned for the wasteful days of youth: a page would last several weeks, until at last the sky-blue was almost submerged by black script, crammed into every last tiny space, a line of figures injected at an extraordinary angle so as not to waste a precious scrap of blue – until at last the page was full, and was discarded with a sigh. In Steiner's mind the slowly reducing height of that once magnificent pile was the spending of his life, page by page. The hand that wrote on that last page would be the senile scrawling of his epitaph.

But for now he crammed Sabine's address and telephone number into a narrow corridor of space in a corner of the blue pad. He stared at the number, toying with an impulse to dial it. She had made no mention of her shoes. He guessed that her pride would not allow it; it was for him now to telephone her.

The shoes were where he had thrown them the night before. The sight of them tormented him. He was no longer angry with her, but could not bear the sight of them. He had a sudden inspiration, picked up the shoes and put them in a bag. Moments later, he knocked on Boris's door.

Boris answered, blinking at Steiner stupidly. His hair was dirty and dishevelled. Steiner's suspicion that he was drunk was confirmed by Boris inviting him in with a ponderous and deliberate gravity. He handed Steiner a drink in silence and Steiner smiled inwardly; he understood that Boris was afraid to ask in case he declined; like all drunks, he desired an accomplice.

Steiner saw that Boris looked at the bag with a knowing look as if he knew what was inside it, and, as in confirmation, he lay his hand heavily but sympathetically on Steiner's shoulder.

"So it's over for you now."

Steiner nodded. He hesitated, torn between the desire to be honest with his friend and a feeling of revulsion at the thought of Boris's sympathy. His persistent image of Boris as a bear conjured a vision of two brown bears rolling on their backs, wailing and roaring in pain, their great paws cuffing at each other in a reflex reaction to their suffering.

He was wary, knowing that Boris might be back in contact with Sabine – how else could he have acquired this knowledge? Perhaps, even, he was her confidant now, duped into reporting Steiner's words. He showed no emotion and was aware of a pair of sharp bear's eyes watching him carefully, animated by some emotion that penetrated the stupor of drink. And he understood: these events had awoken hope in Boris. How pitiful that made him, and how cruel Sabine, if, as he guessed, she used this weakness to manipulate him. The two bears rolling on the ground knew no ill-will towards each other until that slender hand threw a lump of meat to lie on the ground between them; then they surveyed each other with a new suspicion and shrewdness as they saw each other for what they truly were: rivals.

Boris stared at Steiner with drunken introspection. "I'll remember that last night until the day I die. She was cold as ice when she told me. I couldn't believe it had happened – not so suddenly, with no fight or bad words between us. She had decided – that's how she told me – she had decided, and that was it – puff!" He threw his hands upwards and outwards in a gesture that was slowed by his drunkenness, replacing its dramatic effect with comedy. Steiner had to suppress his laughter. Boris continued: *"All over as if it had never been. It seemed so unfair, as if I had done something wrong and not been given the chance to make amends. The more I thought about it, the more I couldn't believe it. I sat up all night to write a letter to her. I couldn't get it right. I tore it up so many times that I had to use my foot to make space in the bin. It was first light when I finished. I managed as best I could to tell her how I loved her, without sounding too trite or clichéd. And when I handed it to her... I'll never forget the look on her face – watchful, like some suspicious little animal, then overwhelmed, like a child who's been given her first bicycle. She held it in her hand as if it was something incredibly precious, and she smiled at me – I'd never seen her smile like that; as if she was shy, incredulous, humbled – but flattered – that's it – flattered – as if to say, 'You did this for me? I can't believe that this is for me?' And then she read it in front of me; I hadn't expected that. I stood there like a condemned man awaiting the pronouncement of my fate – and do you know what she did?"* Boris reached for his drink with a smile that seemed curiously inappropriate to his anguish. *"She scrabbled under the bed, just like a squirrel digging up its winter store, and pulled out an old plastic bag. Then she folded my letter, taking the corners precisely to each other to halve it, then quartered it; and she placed it ever so carefully in the bag as if it was some commendation she'd been given... And you know what?"* Steiner shook his head. *"The bag was full of letters – dozens and dozens of them."*

Boris lapsed into moody drunken silence. Steiner handed the bag of shoes to Boris, explaining that she had left them in his apartment, and that he would be obliged if Boris would return them to her when he next saw her. He was puzzled by Boris's reaction; he appeared suddenly awkward.

"I'm sorry – if you don't mind, I'd rather not take them."

Steiner observed his friend in silence, and made a guess. "What nonsense has she told you?"

Boris's expression of surprise betrayed him. He looked briefly at Steiner and then away. His ungainly body hunched awkwardly – a bear surprised in his lair before a light shining painfully in his eyes.

"She told me you would call. She told me... It's a bit awkward." Boris appeared sullen, as if resentful of being put in this position.

Steiner attempted to reassure him. "You won't hurt my feelings."

"Well – she said you'd taken it badly – she said she didn't want me to be involved – because of our friendship."

Steiner got up, patting his friend gently on the shoulder. He understood the futility of denying this accusation; he remembered the heated arguments they had had about science, and how he had been angered, not by Boris's arrogance – that had been merely irritating – but by his unquestioning acceptance. In this way, Boris was simple, and no match for the guile of Sabine. He laughed inwardly at the irony: he could see how she had manipulated Boris, how her true intent was concerned with Steiner; but he was equally certain that Boris believed the opposite: that her real interest was in him.

Boris shook his head. "That's what she said, but believe me, I make no judgement – I understand – except that..." He looked at Steiner thoughtfully. "You're different from me – I couldn't do what you're doing now – I couldn't part with anything of hers – and I couldn't have left the way you did. She was wrong about that. She thought you'd come crawling back on your hands and knees just as I would have done – but I told her: not Steiner – he's not weak like me – if he says he's gone, then gone he is – he won't be back. And you know what? I was proud of you. It was as if you'd done it for both of us. I prayed that you wouldn't give in."

Steiner paused at the door and looked at the bag. "They can't be so important for her to have left them. I'll put them in the rubbish. Perhaps you'd tell her if you see her."

Boris stared at him in dismay, then clutched suddenly at the bag, holding it to him possessively. His lips trembled with emotion, then, as if ashamed, he muttered a farewell before turning back into his apartment, stumbling awkwardly against the doorframe with his bulky clumsy body bent protectively around the precious bag. He slammed the door shut. Steiner watched after him with the thought that Boris' love for Sabine was somehow more pitiful than his own. Now she had succeeded in separating her two former lovers; this last cruel trick of Steiners', to test his friend, had been her work. The image returned of her snaking dance on that dreadful night – the look of cruel triumph on her face as she enticed the dancers around her with the touch of her body against theirs. But would not that triumph be thwarted when she learnt how Boris had recovered her shoes? He imagined another expression of agitated concentration as she contemplated his actions. Her intelligence would not be deceived, but perhaps her lack of self-confidence would cause her doubt. Steiner was gratified by this thought but was also ashamed; in his desperation to return the hurt of her rejection, he had sacrificed his friendship with Boris; he had joined with her dancers – one who danced warily alone, one who resisted her gravitation but moved in an eccentric orbit dictated by a different rhythm of the same tune.

Steiner's anxiety grew as the day approached to return. The peaceful walks he had planned were spoiled by his preoccupation. On his last day, he returned to the hotel with no memory of where he had been, although he felt from the tiredness of his legs that he must have walked for miles. The confrontation that he had avoided with this break would not long now be delayed. He anticipated it with excitement, joy and dread.

The hotel manager greeted him at the bar with a glass of vodka. Steiner thanked him but chose to avoid his company by taking a seat away from the bar. The man struck him as a rather peculiar character; not an unpleasant fellow and friendly enough in a gruff sort of way, but strangely wary, as if suspecting him of some derangement. Steiner found this annoying. Ever since the night when he had had a bad dream, the man had looked at him dubiously, even doubting the intensity of the storm that he had witnessed with his own eyes.

The bar was empty. Steiner lit a cigarette. His eye was drawn to the flashing lights of a gaming machine, and on a whim he got up to inspect it. Such machines were unfamiliar to him. He inserted some coins hesitantly, bewildered by a multitude of symbols and flashing lights. He played for some minutes, making little sense of the game. He had nearly exhausted his credit when the machine unexpectedly spat out almost double the number of coins he had inserted. He was pleasantly surprised at this, but the machine irritated him. He could guess at the number of symbols on each tumbler from an estimate of the radius of the wheels, and he could calculate the probabilities of a particular sequence occurring; but he suspected that the movements weren't random, and in any case he could not understand the various features which were initiated by certain sequences. He finished his drink and ordered another at the bar, returning to the machine with a new determination to at least understand the infuriating device, even if he couldn't master it.

He played for some time, winning occasionally, twice when he was down to his last credit. The game began to make more sense to him. There was one set of symbols shaped like a crooked 'Z'. These symbols appeared only rarely. His largest win came after two of the symbols appeared together. He searched the key on the front panel and saw that three such symbols would pay an enormous prize, but saw too that there was no key showing the pay out for four of the symbols. This puzzled him; there was an award shown for four of all the other symbols – significantly higher than for three. At first he supposed that the symbols were only included on three of the tumblers, but after some time playing he found that this was incorrect: there was one on each. He considered the possibility that the mechanism of the machine prevented all four from appearing together. Alternatively perhaps there was no prize for four in a row. This thought offended his logic. The idea of the four 'Z's fascinated him and he played on, uninterested in the occasional small wins other than in the opportunity they gave him to continue. Even the massive pay out for three of the symbols did not compel his interest; he wanted to know if it was possible for four of the symbols to appear together, and if so what payout would be the reward.

He pressed the start button and turned away to light a cigarette; and in that moment – as he turned back to the machine – he saw the jagged symbol in the centre of the first tumbler. A second later the same symbol settled with a decisive click into position on the second tumbler. He held his breath. The last two wheels seemed to spin for an unusual length of time, and then, almost simultaneously, they stopped suddenly as if some overriding mechanism had decided on this one chance in 194,481 (as he had calculated). It was as if his thoughts had been read and challenged by the machine. The four motionless and identical symbols aligned defiantly before him and blinked up at him expectantly.

He drew on his cigarette, fascinated. What would happen now? What prize would be paid? But nothing happened. The start button blinked, inviting the next play. He laughed to himself. His question was answered: there was no key for four of the symbols because there was no prize! The deception of this amused him. His hand moved towards the start button. He paused for a moment to savour one last look at this elusive symmetry – and in that moment the machine appeared to go wild; a sequence of lights he had not seen before lit the machine from deep within – the colours of the rainbow radiating from the centre.

He stepped back in amazement. Every panel of the machine was lit with colour; and brightest of all – the focus of the cascade – were the four aligned symbols, flickering like crystals, one colour merging with the next. As he watched, the tumblers turned slowly away, revealing an opaque screen, flecked with the colours of the retreating crystals, dying down like the embers of a fire until the screen was in darkness.

He moved forward, his hands gripping the sides of the machine, wondering with excitement what would happen next. Now all the lights were extinguished; not even the start button was lit. All he could see was his own reflection in the blackness of the screen. He frowned. Was it his reflection? The image in the screen appeared to be outlined in light. The features were turned away from him. The machine lit up with a steady aura of green neon, framing the screen so that it gained the definition of a picture. It was his own silhouette turned away from him. He was bemused. What sort of a game was this – and what sort of prize?

Suddenly the start button began to flash and a caption lit up in a ribbon at the bottom of the screen: 'Press once for jackpot. Press twice for the game of life'. Steiner hesitated. What did this mean – 'game of life'? He resisted the temptation of the jackpot; his curiosity would not be denied; he had to know. He pressed the button firmly twice, anxious that he had hesitated for too long.

The screen illuminated suddenly. From the background definition, He saw that the figure was moving. He wondered if it had just started to move, or if he had only just become aware of the movement due to the illumination of the screen. He saw that the figure was seated in the back of a vehicle. A driver sat in front, hunched over a steering wheel. The movement came from the passage of the vehicle along a tarmac highway that opened up before them, lit with blue mercury lights glowing through the side windows as the vehicle passed by.

He gripped the side of the machine and, as he did so, the vehicle appeared to increase in speed: he was controlling the motion of the vehicle. He found that by concentrating he could accelerate, slow and turn the vehicle; the hunched silhouette of the driver turned the wheel at his will.

He concentrated on the road. It was a busy duel-carriageway with patches of weeds in the centre. He recognised it as one of the transit-routes out of Berlin. The vehicles were old. He was overcome with a sense of familiarity as if of a distant memory that would have gone forever if not awoken by this image. He had travelled this road as a young child on a journey with his father; but the memory was so ephemeral that he was uncertain if it had been a real journey or a dream.

He had to concentrate to steer the vehicle even though the road was almost straight. It was as if the driver with his back to him in the front seat was fighting with him for control. Illuminated buildings appeared in the driver's mirror, and suddenly Steiner knew the direction of this journey. These were the tower blocks of West Berlin, not the bombed-out shells that lay in ruins in the eastern sector of the city. This was, as he had supposed, one of the transit-routes: the central route from Drewitz to Marienborn, but his destination lay off to the right, to Brandenburg – the place of his birth.

He became aware of a distraction somewhere off the screen. He glanced upwards to see a line of miniature silhouettes of himself. The first three in the line were crossed through with the jagged 'Z' symbol, and the last of these three flashed with red light momentarily before turning to black. He had to return his attention to the screen, fearful of what would happen if he lost control of the vehicle. As he did so, the hunched figure of the driver turned towards him. Steiner recognised the leering evil in the face turned towards him with an unpleasant shock; it was the man he had encountered at the Interhotel. The face spoke with mocking malevolence.

"Three lives gone; four left. You'll turn back if you value your life."

Steiner felt sweat break out on his forehead. Why had he pressed the button twice? Fool! Now he understood the 'game of life'. He had no idea of his reward for winning, but he understood now the penalty for losing.

A familiar turning opened up to the right. He must trust

to this distant memory. He willed the vehicle to slow and turn. The driver, turned away from him now, grunted as if with reluctance, but the vehicle made the turn. Steiner felt a momentary relief at the familiarity of this place. The tarmac gave way to cobblestones. There were woods to the left, fields to the right and, across them, a glimpse of a town and the famous lake.

He glanced upwards. Five silhouettes were now crossed though by the jagged symbols. He gripped the sides of the machine and the vehicle accelerated, hurtling towards the town at a dangerous pace. The lake appeared to the left. A sixth symbol blinked red. Steiner relaxed his grip. The vehicle slowed to a halt. The driver opened the door, his face contorted by an expression of vicious hatred. Steiner ran into the courtyard of the old house. In spite of his fear, his cheeks were wet with tears at the precious memories of this place. He was at the door. He understood the prize now. His hand was on the catch.

"Herr Steiner – Herr Steiner."

The game receded – the room, the screen; the reels returned but were in darkness. The manager was at his side.

"I'm closing the bar now. Would you like a night-cap – on the house?"

Steiner stared at the lifeless machine and saw that the manager had switched it off. He opened his mouth to protest but hesitated; he could not explain the nature of the prize he had been playing for – and as for the jackpot... He saw the four symbols in the darkness; they were all different.

He accepted the manager's invitation. He felt exhausted. The manager's hospitality extended to two glasses of vodka before Steiner took himself to bed.

The telephone was ringing as Steiner returned from work the next day. His hand shook as he reached for the receiver. He was shocked at the strength of his disappointment as he answered to a man's voice; a wave of desolation and loneliness swept over him. The voice introduced itself as,

Max – a friend of Sabine. He sounded surprised when Steiner told him that she no longer lived there. He asked for her number. Steiner stared at the blue pad in front of him; his hand reached out subconsciously and possessively towards it. He had never heard of this confident and cultured young man before. His thoughts accused: "I don't believe in you, my friend." He contrived to make his reply sound casual without being uncivil: "I'm sorry, I don't have her number." He replaced the receiver without giving the man any opportunity to reply. The thought of this charade, in which he had been a momentary player, was intensely shameful to him. He saw himself as he had seen Boris: a performing bear, dancing pathetically on his back legs, driven by the whip of his mistress. He found that he had unconsciously torn the top sheet of paper from the pad; it lay crumpled it in his hand. He threw it suddenly, violently and contemptuously away as if it burnt into his flesh. He was certain of the deception behind this call, and guessed at its motivation: to demonstrate that she had eligible young men seeking after her whereabouts? To sting him with a reminder of her presence and ensure that she was in the foreground of his thoughts? But more certainly: she would want to know if he had kept her number – and soon she would know that he had not. This thought was his only solace: just as with the dancing shoes, he would not play her game. He determined that from that moment on, he would not answer the telephone.

Steiner's return journey was uneventful apart from one peculiar and disturbing incident. He disembarked from the train at Magdeburg and caught a bus that stopped outside the laboratory complex. The past week seemed like a dream that had intervened in the reality he faced now. She was near now, and their meeting was inevitable. His anxiety returned. The excitement he had felt at times in anticipation of this encounter was now replaced by misery. He knew as a certainty that she would be unchanged by the years: her beauty was incorruptible. But he was equally certain that whatever image she had retained of him in her memory would be shattered by the reality of seeing him. He was absorbed by this thought as he made his way around a tree-lined avenue skirting the perimeter of the complex towards his apartment. He became conscious of a movement amongst the trees in front of him. Something white flapped amongst the green foliage. He quickened his pace. As he grew nearer, he reddened with anger and outrage, running towards the dreadful scene before him. A little white and tan terrier hung struggling from the bough of a tree, suspended by a rope around its neck. Steiner gave a roar of rage and broke into a run. It was a race against time. The little beast convulsed frantically: it must still be alive, he might yet be in time. What sort of a monster could commit such an atrocity? Steiner had never known such rage. If he could find the culprit, he would strangle him with his bare hands. As he reached the place, Steiner saw that he was too late; the poor creature hung lifeless, his large brown eyes bulging and bloodshot, rimmed with unexpectedly long lashes like white whiskers. Steiner's eyes filled with tears. He wiped at them with his sleeve, and suddenly the little dog was gone. He wiped his eyes properly with a handkerchief and blinked to clear them. Not only was the little dog gone, but the place had changed. There was no overhanging branch; in fact the nearest tree was some distance away. He turned back to the path. His legs felt weak.

The telephone calls continued. Steiner maintained his resolve not to answer them. He would freeze at the sound of the incessantly ringing bell before approaching the instrument cautiously, drawn to it inexorably, watching its inanimate form in silence for a long time before he could bring himself to leave it. At first he felt elation at having conquered his weakness. But after many nights of this repeated ritual, he came to realise that he was still enslaved, still one of her harem of dancers. Revolving in an outer orbit, with no hope of the glancing touch of her body against his, lent no serenity to his dance; it was as frenzied and desperate as ever. This thought angered him. He would not let her ruin his life. He decided to resume his social life so that he would be out when the telephone rang.

In the coming days and weeks he occupied himself with visits to friends, dinner parties, trips to the cinema and concerts in Magdeburg. Not one evening was left without an engagement, and rarely did he return home before midnight. It seemed that this frenetic occupation slowly bought about the desired effect: he thought about her less often and she was slowly expelled from his dreams. But then one night his slowly reconstructed calm was demolished in a single blow.

He returned home late from dinner at the Schellenbergs'. He felt her presence from the moment he let himself in the door; every room was alive with her memory as if her ghost danced around him. In the dining room, her long elegant form leant against the mantelpiece, staring directly into his eyes, the trouble of their conversation showing in furrows on her forehead. In the sitting room, she hunched over her record player, playing and re-playing the dissonant piece of music that would haunt him forever. And in the bedroom, she lay on the bed, her arms reaching out for him as she told him she loved him. The memories were so strong that he imagined he could smell her perfume.

His torment continued in his dreams. They danced together in the dance hall, her snaking figure almost touching him but eluding his hands that sought to hold her to him. They walked together, his hand held out to hers, almost, but not quite, touching. Then, somehow, they became parted and it was her hand held out to him, but he could not take it as some force drove her away – her long slender hand receding into darkness. He followed her retreating figure, guided by the chimes of her locket. He knew now that he was dreaming and was unsurprised to find her there beside him. He smelt her perfume. His arms were around her. Only then did he awake to find her gone. His eyes were blurred with tears. He sat up in bed, fighting back the heaving sobs that shook him *uncontrollably. He breathed deeply in an attempt to master this paroxysm, still held by the realism of his departing dreams and still breathing in her perfume. This puzzled him; he was awake now. He snatched up the pillow beside him; the scent increased, and he understood: the perfume was in the pillow just as it was all around the apartment. He held the pillow to his face. She must have kept a key and let herself in. He was amazed rather than angry. She must have watched his movements, waited until he had gone out for the evening, and then let herself in. He recognised the mood in which she had done this: reckless, abandoned and occupied with inner conversations.*

He let himself into his apartment with apprehension and excitement. The doormat was covered with letters. He was both relieved and disappointed to find that none were from her. One was from Hirsch. This in itself was surprising, Hirsch rarely wrote letters. The message was characteristically illegible and curt, asking Steiner to telephone as soon as he returned.

The telephone rang and he froze. His legs almost failed under him. He sank into a chair and picked up the receiver. It was Hirsch. He sounded irritated, which was not unusual; and worried, which was.

"Didn't you get my message?"

Steiner laughed. He had always found Hirsch's abruptness an endearing trait, and it was good to hear his voice again.

"Well, here I am – did you miss me so badly?"

"Wondered where you'd been – we all have."

Steiner was puzzled. "I took leave at short notice."

There was a long pause before Hirsch replied: "I see. It might have been an idea to tell someone – me for instance."

Steiner was amused. "Of course I told people. I've been across the border; I had to tell people to get a visa. I know I'm not quite the indispensable member of your staff that I used to be, but I wouldn't just wander off without telling anyone."

Hirsch sounded surprised. "Our people I meant." His tone retained its gruffness but softened. "No matter – as long as you're all right."

Steiner replaced the receiver chuckling at this last remark. He unpacked his case. In spite of his earlier apprehension he was relieved to be back home. For some reason he couldn't recall the events of the last few days clearly just now, other than vague memories of disturbed nights and lonely days. He looked forwards to his return to work and reunion with his colleagues. He poured himself a glass of vodka and settled in his favourite chair.

He had the lock changed on the door to his apartment. Every day after work he came home in a state of anticipation, expecting to find some signs of her presence, perhaps a letter, but there was nothing.

After two weeks had passed he began to think that she had finally broken all contact. Knowing the pace of her life, he expected that she had met someone else by now. He imagined sourly how this new man would be targeted by her intense obsessive attention. He found himself pitying and yet envying this imagined lover.

And then, at that special time on that special day, just as light was fading, the telephone rang. His resolve not to answer was overwhelmed. He had forgotten the affect of her voice. A hand squeezed his heart.

She was concerned that she had not paid her share of the bills; it was important to her to do this. Her voice was apparently calm but he was undeceived; he recognised the mild hysteria that underlay her words. He told her that the bills only added up to a small amount; they had long since been paid, and it was of no consequence. She appeared to accept his reply. Her voice changed to the soft intimate tone she had used when they had been together; she asked him how he was. This struck him as peculiarly inappropriate and he replied shortly and coldly. She finished the conversation abruptly. Steiner knew that he had been the cause of this and regretted for a moment that he had not responded to her advance; but this moment soon passed and was replaced with anger: if she had changed her mind and regretted her rejection of him, then it was for her to say so directly.

He paced the room, smoking absent-mindedly, running through all the haughty and dignified responses he wished he had thought of at the time. It seemed only moments later that there was a knock on the door.

The reality of her presence disarmed him. He could only stammer an invitation to come in. She smiled at his awkwardness. They sat facing each other. She looked into his eyes affectionately, apparently unaffected by their meeting. This knowledge oppressed him; he could scarcely meet her eyes.

Her conversation was commonplace for a while; she told him of the apartment she had taken and the doings of the neighbours. Then her eyes and her voice softened and she repeated the question she had asked earlier: how was he getting on? She spoke with tenderness as if she really cared.

She insisted on leaving him a small amount of money. Steiner looked at the twenty-mark note after she had gone and was amused; it was an absurdly small amount of money, but typical of her, he thought – she dealt in tokens. Her true purpose was a mystery to him and occupied his mind for a long time after she had left. There was nothing of any importance in their conversation, and it seemed to him that she had little interest in telling her news or hearing his. It took him a while to reach his conclusion: she had just wanted to see him, to look at him. Her motive eluded him, although it had evidently been important enough to justify the panic that he suspected had driven her to make this visit. And yet it seemed that this encounter had satisfied her... Satisfied! That was the elusive impression that he had been searching for; it was as if she had fulfilled some need just by seeing him. When they had parted she had seemed at peace. He regretted having given her this satisfaction; for him the meeting had brought only profound disturbance; her beauty had reawakened his craving for her that had been dulled by their time apart. He should not have answered the telephone or opened the door to her. Why should he provide her with the peace of mind that she denied him? Her farewell had been careless, as if she was already preoccupied with her life, which in those brief moments had moved irrevocably away from him. He was certain now that he would never see her again.

He retired to bed, pleasantly tired. His eyes closed; his thoughts wandered. He was on the edge of sleep when he heard a familiar sound – so faint that at first he thought it was his imagination: the distant chiming tune of her locket. He sat up in bed. The tune receded and then intensified; it approached from the back alleys until it stopped directly opposite his window. His heart, beating to the rhythm, seemed to throb in his chest. His emotions tumbled to the tune: gratitude – she had preserved his memory as truly as he had hers; yearning – to run out to her and embrace her; but overwhelming all, fear – she would recoil at the reality of his physical deterioration; or perhaps seeing him once more would satisfy that strange need in her, just as it had all that time before, and she would depart finally from his life. He dare not let her see him again; he turned his head into his pillow to blot out the sound of the chimes that called to him. Tears of self-pity poured down his cheeks.

The sound of the chimes persisted in his dreams. He stood alone on a beach, working at the string of a kite that flew up to a tremendous height. Waves tumbled noiselessly on the sands, whipped up by a breeze from out to sea. He saw the faces of his friends in the rolling crests – Schellenberg, Sylvie, Hirsch, Ulrika and Boris. The waves broke on a white figure. It was Sabine – her body stretched out, her drowned face turned towards him. The receding tide drained away, leaving her beached and alone.

He awoke with a memory of the dream. As he dressed for work he glanced casually at his watch and was amazed to find that it was nearly mid-day; he never overslept on a working day. He rang his department to tell them that he had overslept.

It was pleasant to be back amongst his colleagues, but the joyous reunion he had envisaged was subdued in reality; his colleagues were affable enough but they seemed too busy to have time for anything more than a perfunctory greeting.

He sat at his desk and tried to recall his work. His mind was almost a complete blank. He knew that it was just one of those temporary memory blocks and that if he concentrated for a moment it would pass. But concentrating proved to be difficult and he began to feel frustrated. Why was everyone so busy this morning? This was what had flustered him: his colleagues' unnecessary preoccupation with their work. Was it really so vital that they could not afford a few seconds to chat with their boss? Since when had he been so aloof that he had no time to pass the time of day with them? Were they not all supposed to be comrades? He began to feel quite worked-up; no wonder he couldn't concentrate. As if to emphasise the point, a young technician came running through the door carrying a sheaf of papers. Steiner frowned; no one ever ran; it was dangerous, in fact it was forbidden; also – and this was more the cause of his irritation – it was completely unnecessary. He snapped at the youth:

"Hey, you! Slow down – you know running isn't allowed – what's the rush?"

The boy seemed suddenly to switch position from where he was already receding from Steiner to directly in front of him. He appeared absurdly surprised. Steiner found this even more irritating. The boy muttered some ridiculous protest, denied even that he had been running. What was the point of that when Steiner had seen him with his own eyes? And besides, it wasn't a capital crime. He dismissed the boy by turning contemptuously to his desk, and was not surprised to find his notes missing; everything seemed unbearably trying this morning. He was pleased, moments later, when Hirsch appeared and called him into his office. Steiner forgot his irritation; he was always pleased to see Hirsch.

But his irritability returned at the sight of his old friend: even the calm stoical Hirsch appeared tense and anxious. It was as if the whole department was infected by some ludicrous neurosis.

"Not you as well – what is wrong with everyone today? Rushing around looking so anxious as if there'll be some dreadful calamity if they so much stop to pass the time of day – what's wrong with the place? And where's my work? Some numbskull's cleared my desk."

Hirsch's frown was mildly aggressive. Steiner recognised this as the affect of awkwardness on an honest nature.

"I've passed it over – had to do it – sorry. Your work…" for once Hirsch's bluntness was restrained, "is not up to standard." He peered at Steiner, took off his spectacles and stared down at them. "Is something wrong?"

Steiner was now seriously alarmed. It was true that his work seemed to have been unusually burdensome of late; it had been difficult to concentrate since he had heard the news of her return. But he was mortified to think that this had caused a problem for his old friend. He owed Hirsch an immediate explanation and an apology.

Hirsch listened in apparent surprise, interrupting only at the mention of Sabine. "The girl you were with all that time ago? The one I met?"

"Yes – yes." This was a pleasant memory to Steiner.

"And she's come back?"

Steiner opened his mouth to reply, but at this moment he caught Hirsch's unguarded expression which shocked him profoundly: it was twisted with a sly predatory lust. Steiner was appalled. He continued the conversation with half his mind occupied. He was relieved to see his friend's usual expression return. Perhaps some trick of the light had exaggerated that grimace, but Hirsch had always been an incorrigible womaniser, and Sabine had encouraged him; he remembered Sylvie telling him this. He was alerted from his muse by an expression of discomfort that now animated Hirsch's features.

"I've spoken to the staff director – we could put you down as sick."

Steiner frowned in confusion. "Sick? I'm sorry, Hirsch, I wasn't listening properly – why should you put me down as sick?"

Hirsch busied himself filling his pipe. "I'm not a doctor – I don't know what it is – overwork is the latest nonsense; seems like an excuse to me, but..." He looked up at Steiner mildly. "Not you – that's not you. I'm no good at this, Steiner – you're an old friend – a good brain – and a freethinker – always respected you – you, Schellenberg, some of the others. We've always talked straight – can't change a habit... Your work's rubbish – has been for some time. That's what I've been trying to say to you. You can go sick, at least for a while, or you can retire early. You'd better think about it."

Steiner nodded as if understanding but he was in turmoil. Evidently Hirsch did not accept the explanation he had given him and he found this deeply hurtful; his work may have suffered to some extent, but how could it have been rubbish? It was not like his friend to exaggerate like this; but then again, Steiner had never seen that dreadful expression on his face before. It was a terrible thought, but perhaps Hirsch had an ulterior motive in this; perhaps he was jealous at the prospect of Sabine's return; perhaps he wanted her for himself.

Steiner did not understand how profoundly this conversation had shocked him until some time later. As if awakening from a dream, he looked around him and was surprised to find himself on his way home in the middle of the afternoon. He had no recollection of leaving Hirsch's office, returning to his desk, or lunching in the refectory, although he did not feel hungry, so presumably he had done so. He even had a strange feeling that this had all happened yesterday, although he knew this could not be so, since it was now afternoon; and besides, the hurt and upset he felt was fresh in his mind; his hands trembled and he felt light-headed. Even after he had reached his apartment and poured himself a glass of vodka these feeling persisted. He was also exhausted; he found himself catnapping, awaking unrefreshed at intervals, with memories of disturbing dreams.

It was night when he awoke fully. The tremors in his hands had increased. He poured himself another glass of vodka. He knew that he had been dreaming of Sabine; the aura of her was around him. Although he could not recall any details of the dream, he guessed that it was connected with her dreadful past because he was left with a particular mixture of sympathy and horror – but also romance, for that episode in her life was so intimately a part of her.

He became gradually aware of a distant sound invading the silence: the chiming tune that announced her approach. He was drawn to the window by the sound. A full moon lit the back alleys and the pastures beyond with startling silver. The tune was appallingly loud, but as he scanned the empty alleyways it retreated. She was out there, somewhere in the shadows; he could picture her head bent forward, concentrating intently on the locket. The unseen hands, lit by the moonlight, would be lined with age but still beautiful. Did they shake with a fine tremor of anticipation? Or were they still? And the expression in her eyes stooped over them – did she brood, smile, or mock?

He looked up to the moon, so startlingly bright that he suspected it of some connection with the unearthly tune that waxed and waned as if it were the waters of the earth. He had never known it so bright; never noticed before how its continents and oceans were shaped as the earth's. Its brightness stung his eyes and he drew back into the room. The chimes intensified. He looked around, afraid – what trick was this? The sound was within the room. His eyes alighted with a shock of fear on the illuminated dial of his radio. How could this be? He had not switched the set on. He approached it warily; the tune increased with each step. He reached for the volume dial. He turned it up by mistake and the volume increased unbearably. He twisted the dial in the opposite direction but the chimes only changed their tone to a deeper bell-like quality without diminishing in volume. The sound was now harsh and dissonant. He twisted frantically at the tuning dial and was relieved to hear the tune dissolve into static; then, as the dial turned, he heard a brief burst of another melody: beautiful, insistent, and familiar. He turned the dial back but the slightest touch tuned into the music and past it. Try as he would, he could not tune the dial finely enough. He used both hands to make the minutest adjustment, but with each attempt the music returned only for a tantalising moment. He crouched down to inspect the radio and understood his difficulty: there was another much smaller tuning dial for fine tuning – strange that he had never noticed it before; he turned it and the music grew steadily clearer until it was perfectly tuned-in. It was the most wonderful melody; his heart sang at the beauty of it. Now he understood the feeling of familiarity: it was the music he had heard in the hotel, performed by the same musician.

He sat on the floor, caught up in a great tide of emotion that carried him up and swept him along with such force that he was afraid. The beauty of the music was cut with pain. It darkened and intensified, passing beyond the point of familiarity. He understood now why the musician in the hotel bar had put down his instrument: the music was too deep, intense and powerful to be listened to safely; it inspired emotions that possessed, damaged and maddened.

The intricacy of the piece intensified with the addition of more instruments. New rhythms spiralled chaotically away from the core and returned. Harmonies merged, weaving in and out of phase, and palpitated his heart by induction.

And suddenly he recognised the nature of this music, knew that he stood on the very threshold of life, to be swept over and away – but he leant forward towards the dancing illumination of the dial, embracing the beauty of destruction that cascaded through his soul. And just as he thought he could bear no more, the music began to subside.

He reached out a trembling hand towards the dial, searching for the signal that ebbed slowly away. But in spite of his efforts the music faded into distant space and was replaced by a mocking hum. He spun the dial desperately across the band, but the background was broken only by spitting static, until at last a distant echo of music began to return. His heart leapt with relief, but only for a moment as a wild coarse melody of raucous fiddles swelled slowly in volume.

He sprang back from the set in fear; the music was around him and behind him – accompanied by shouting and mocking laughter. A clap of hands made him spin around. The musicians were there in his room. He stared directly at them – a family of gypsies – a raven haired woman with a scarlet head-scarf and face, an impudent looking child with his head thrown back and his mouth open in mocking song, and an evil-looking fellow with missing teeth who raked his bow fiercely across the bridge of a fiddle.

Anger overtook his fear. He would not stand for this in his own apartment. He was startled by the sound of his voice over the terrible music. "Get out – this instant – all of you!" The words sounded ridiculous and he was not surprised to see the mocking laughter in their faces as they turned on him.

He was awoken by a distant banging that reverberated strangely in his ears. He raised his head: his room was in a terrible state, the curtains were torn and pulled away from the rail, his clothes were strewn around all over the place – and, to his dismay, he saw his radio-set – one of his most precious possessions – lying on the floor with its tuning-knob twisted off. Who had done this? Someone was banging on the door. Perhaps it was the police – his apartment had obviously been broken into. He raised himself off the bed and was surprised to find that he was dressed and facing the wrong way. His head throbbed; he must have drunk too much. The banging on the door persisted. It was the urgency of the knocking that alerted him; he recognised that panicky mood that would not be denied. He found himself in the hallway pressed tightly against the wall. There was another flurry of knocking on the door. He longed to run to the door and dreaded the moment when the knocking would cease and she would turn away; but his legs felt weak; he could feel his heartbeat singing in his ears... He was not ready.

Sylvie Schellenberg died suddenly and unexpectedly. Schellenberg found himself surrounded by friends. Being a modest man, he had no idea of how much these friends cared for him or, curiously, for his wife. There was much concern among them for how he would cope; the eccentricity of that devoted scientific mind was easily mistaken for instability – but this was illusory. Schellenberg did not collapse; he withdrew a little, but he was already so remote that the change was barely noticeable. The only outward sign of concern to his friends was that he continued to speak of his wife in the present tense.

Steiner and Hirsch spent the evening before the funeral with Schellenberg. Conversation turned safely to science. Steiner and Hirsch indulged their friend, or so they thought, debating theories of astro-physics until the early hours. The two friends concealed their discomfort at this surreal conversation, and were relieved, as they all got up to leave, to hear Schellenberg say: "I miss her so badly. I can say it in front of you two." He broke down and wept uncontrollably, without shame or care.

When Schellenberg was recovered, they all clasped hands at the door, each miserable, but comforted by the true love and comradeship that existed between them.

The next day, when helping with the funeral preparations, Steiner noticed a large and extraordinarily inappropriate wreath: an elaborate display of roses, tulips, carnations and orchids; it would have been flamboyant for a wedding, it was grotesque for a funeral. He wondered afterwards what had caused him to open the attached note – perhaps a subconscious recognition of her mark? He read the inscription with amazement..."Dearest Sylvie, I can speak to you in death in a way that I would not have dared in life. We could have been sisters – I knew that after our one brief encounter; circumstances alone made it impossible. How much I regret that. But we will find each other in the next life and we will be sisters. In loving memory – Sabine."

That single final word in her flourishing but precise script caused him to sway on his feet. He read and reread the extraordinary message. Sabine had only met Sylvie on that one occasion and had discerned her disapproval. Could those words be sincere? Did she truly feel kinship and understanding? Did she truly forgive and regret? Or was this the mocking, vengeful triumph of the living over the dead? And what was the purpose of this message, written in the knowledge that it could not be received by the one addressed? Were these words murmurs from the heart, or were they written with design over the living?

His questions were answered at the funeral. He stood with Hirsch and Schellenberg at the edge of the open grave as the mortal remains of Sylvie Schellenberg were laid to the earth under a bright afternoon sun. His head was bowed down, a momentary humour lightening his misery: aware at that moment that his hands were clasped firmly, on one side by Schellenberg, and on the other by Hirsch. He was transported back to a time before adulthood, before such physical contact had passed out of habit; and in the impish mood that had attended that time, he felt a strong urge to giggle at the absurdity of three mature professors holding hands together.

He looked up to see Sabine staring intently into his eyes. His shock was so great that he was almost paralysed by a sudden weakness. A thought flashed through his mind: what if he had lost his balance and fallen into the open grave to land on top of Sylvie? He found that his right hand had reached out involuntarily. Sabine's expression changed in an instant; she smiled. He tucked his hand safely into his pocket and lowered his gaze to the coffin at his feet. But he forgot for the moment all thought of Sylvie; his mind was occupied with what he had momentarily surprised on Sabine's face: an emotion that shocked him almost as much as her physical presence, an expression as inappropriate as her wreath: envy!

He was shamelessly oblivious to the ceremony around him. The expression of gravity on his face was disconnected from the burial rites being performed in front of him; it was concerned with this inner revelation. What was there here to inspire envy? His first thought was of Sylvie. There was a twisted logic whereby Sabine could resent the love and affection for the dead woman expressed in every face around her grave. But suddenly he understood the fault in his explanation: he was using his logic and not hers; the love and affection around the grave was not just for the dead woman, it existed between the living as well as the dead. This was the true friendship that was denied to Sabine because of her nature that Schellenberg had so aptly likened to the chaos in the universe: either imploding or exploding but never in equilibrium. The only lasting friendship she had known was with Maria, and from what he knew of that, it depended on an unhealthy domination from which she sought liberation.

He was certain he was correct; that brief glimpse into her eyes had discerned an expression that was more complicated than a single emotion. The compound of envy was in solution with its comprising elements; hunger was the attractive force, and contempt its counterbalance to protect her. This peculiar mix could have no other explanation.

He looked up to find her gone.

He knew now the purpose of the wreath; its bizarre message was indeed for the living and not the dead. Decent emotion stirred within him; her behaviour was outrageous, gloating and self-obsessed; but above all he condemned her appalling manipulation of those in the extremity of their distress.

But even as he succeeded for a moment in feeling disgust for her, he yielded to the image of her beauty and magnificence. Even though he deplored her mockery of Sylvie's memory, he could not help admiring her anarchy. He was reminded of those dreadful stories about her father, and the pride with which she had related them - how like him she was. She had smiled at him. How comfortable she was in this role, circling like a lone wolf around a camp-fire, attracted by the light but staying safely away from the flames; perhaps not a wolf – a feral dog that could not bear domestication, and had reverted to the wild. Did he imagine that she had beckoned with her smile, and invited him to join with her? And at that moment he made a choice – between the decency embodied in the corpse at his feet and the intoxicating chaos he imagined was offered to him. His teeth clenched with resolve and yet his heart whimpered at the cruelty of this decision, like a dog – this a different dog – whipped into reluctant obedience by its master.

He found himself slumped on the floor with his back to the wall. He had lost track of time. It was dark now and she had gone. All was silent. Standing up, he was alarmed at the weakness of his legs. He felt a moment of panic; he couldn't go on like this. It would be better to get the encounter over with. She would be back; she might not even wait until morning; she had always been nocturnal and now that she had made the decision to confront him she would not wait. He poured himself a glass of vodka to steady his nerves. He must be ready for her this time. He hurried into his bedroom and got out his best suit. He fumbled with the buttons but at last he was dressed. He braced himself for an inspection in the mirror with a swig of vodka. The face looking back at him was wild-eyed and dishevelled. He was appalled at the stubble on his chin; he must have forgotten to shave. He busied himself with this task but as he turned on the hot tap, the sound of running water was infused with a distant melody. He stood still, straining his ears for the sound that was so faint that he wondered at first if it was his imagination. The gurgling tap altered the sound of the chiming tune to a peculiar and portentous clanging, like a church-bell ringing under water.

His face stared back at him in the mirror. He couldn't face her like this; he needed time to prepare himself mentally as well as physically; he needed a bath, a drink and a good night's sleep. But the chimes were closer now; they approached along the back-alleys, and this time he knew she would not be denied.

He turned from the room, pausing only to grab a bottle of vodka. He slipped down the stairs, feeling his way to the front door in the darkness. And then he was out and running, slowing only when his apartment was out of sight and the sound of the chimes had subsided into silence.

He found himself on the path to the switching station, reaching it with relief, as if it offered sanctuary. He swigged at the bottle of vodka and his nerves calmed. She would find his apartment empty. It was lucky he had heard her approach. What would she do? He must wait for a while; give himself time to think. He felt no cold. Fatigue swept over him.

He heard and saw nothing of Sabine for some time. Every week, at that special time, he found himself checking out of the windows and listening for the telephone. His senses were heightened at that time without any conscious awareness of the day or hour; the lengthening shadow crept into his brain until the critical point was reached and Pavlov rang his bell.

The telephone calls restarted – always at that special time, and always silent. There would be a click as the receiver was replaced, but sometimes this was preceded by a pause. And Steiner, with the resolve he had found at the funeral, would answer with a curt, "Hello?" sometimes adding with affected irritation: "Who is this?" even though his heart pleaded with him to give an alternative response: "Sabine – I know it's you – you don't have to speak – just listen if that's that you want – I'll understand." He ran through a multitude of imaginary conversations; but all ended with the silence at the other end breaking down: "I miss you. Please let's end this and be together again."

This went on for numerous weeks; then came a turning

point. One day his resolve broke: he could not replace the receiver and sat in the half-darkness for what seemed an age, listening to the faintest sound of her breathing before the electronic click announced that the instrument had been replaced – and he had broken into a fit of uncontrollable sobbing. This revealed to him how he had been deceiving himself. He bought an answering machine, and stopped answering the telephone.

The calls persisted for a time, but the line went dead as soon as the machine cut in. Finally the calls ceased and he understood how hope had lived on in his heart; this loss of contact came as a crushing blow.

He got up from the stone path. He must have fallen asleep. He was shaking with cold. He must go back. He approached by the back alleys, keeping to the shadows. He heard the sound of music before his apartment was in sight. He pressed himself back against a wall, his heart pounding. The apartment was flooded with light, the windows open and the curtains flowing out as if blown by the music from within – the dissonant music she had played on the day she had left.

He shivered with the cold; he could not face her, but he could not stay. A freezing mist obscured the ground beneath him. Dawn was still some hours away and he had nowhere to go. It was unthinkable to wake Schellenberg or Hirsch at this hour, and even were he to do so he would only postpone his return – and she would be there, waiting. He had been right: she was committed now to force a confrontation. He turned back, shivering with cold and trepidation, retracing his steps along the dark alleys, out into the streets, moving out of darkness onto a paved way, across shimmering pools of mercury lights stretched before him like stepping stones across a lake. He was relieved to turn off and be once more in darkness. He made his way towards the obscurity of the wasteland. A gleam of light caught his eye and he stopped still, transfixed in wonder. The derelict church he had passed so many times was ablaze with light. Its windows were unboarded; light shone spectacularly through the magnificent stained glass – all shades of red, yellow and green. The doors were flung open, revealing a porch lit with glowing golden icons of the crucifixion set into alcoves. Above the portal, a silver cross caught the light from within and reflected the colours of the rainbow in shades of silver. The deep rumble of an organ was accompanied by muffled chanting.

He moved on, chuckling to himself at the thought of this extraordinary secret that had been hidden from him for so long. He had heard of such things in the GDR, where worship was discouraged, but had never suspected this of all places, so apparently full of unbelievers, of harbouring a Christian underground. If he was to enter and mingle amongst the congregation, how many faces would he recognise? Perhaps even Hirsch and Schellenberg were amongst them. His anxieties were lightened by amusement at this thought. He felt warm again; it was comforting to know that there were others furtively abroad in the night, just as he.

But this comfort deserted him as he approached the low-lit avenue. He could not go back. It was the sight of the switching-station before him that gave him the idea for a desperate solution: the only escape from his situation.

He gathered up dried grass and flammable debris. He pulled down some staves from an old fence, breaking them over his knees into short lengths. His first match caught. He fed the first hesitant flames with the grass and then the wood.

He stood back with satisfaction; but he was afraid – he had never broken the law before. The flames were rising now. Someone would see. The police would be called: perhaps even the military due to the sensitive nature of this establishment. He was sorry for the trouble he would cause, but embraced the thought – they would take him away and she would not be able to find him.

The flames were now roaring up the side of the transformer, catching at the cracked paint.

He knew from a peculiar feeling of weakness that the letter was connected with her. He resisted his first impulse to rip it open. It was addressed in a flowing scrawl in a woman's hand – but not hers. It was post-marked from Potsdam and addressed to 'The old misery'. This was what had paused him; he understood the trap almost at once. Although this was not a familiar nickname, it was designed to sound as if it could be a playful address from some leg-pulling friend. But he knew that none of his friends would use such a puerile name, and was certain that the deliberate ambiguity of the title was merely a design to entice him into opening the letter.

He took the letter to a light but could not see what was inside; he turned it over in his hands, considering all the possibilities. Perhaps the letter would suppose to be intended for her, from some friend perhaps, under the guise of not knowing she had moved – but would contain information truly intended for him. He mused on this for some time, considering other possibilities, but returning to this one as the most likely. What then could this information be? If he knew this, he would know what to do with the letter. A likely answer occurred to him almost at once: she was to be married. He surprised himself by the careless contempt with which he examined this thought. In part, the cheapness of the trick he suspected made him feel superior, but underlying this was another cynicism: the idea of Sabine being married was darkly humorous. Just as the destructive force of an explosive is magnified several times by its containment in a steel case, so would such a union result in her rapid and disastrous insurrection.

He flipped the letter over so that the address faced him again, studying the feminine script. There was of course a simpler explanation: that it was addressed to him in a whimsical submissive mood, using another's hand in the knowledge that he might return it unopened if it were in hers. And inside would be a letter from her to him. It was this possibility that finally decided him against throwing the letter on the fire or returning it unopened. He ripped it open. It contained a ten-mark note and a letter. He read:

"Dearest Sabine, you rotten thing! Where are you? We were all expecting you and you never showed up. Why didn't you call? I will only forgive you when I hear your explanation; I'll not pretend it wasn't a brilliant party – your conscience must be troubling you sufficiently without me loading more onto it!!! Really miss you, darling – and although you don't deserve it, here's a little something for your birthday – it's not imaginative but I know you're short! Ring me as soon as you get this. Even though you are OLD now – and a MISERY, I still send all my love – Monika."

Steiner read and reread the letter. His feeling of contempt expressed as a satisfied smile. How she had revealed her desperation – and lowered herself – to contrive this. He had never heard her mention any friend by this name. She would have to be a truly intimate friend to have been impressed into this deceit. He suspected that Monika did not exist and that her true name was Maria. The intent was obvious: the enclosure of cash would ensure his reply; he would be forced by decency – the one persuasion she could be sure of – into contacting her.

The transformer was now engulfed in flames. A cooling pipe had ruptured with the heat, and spat orange plumes of burning oil up into the night. Pipework creaked as it buckled. Steiner watched, mesmerised. The coiled pipes of the transformer appeared alive with movement, writhing and heaving in all directions. He found this movement irritating; it seemed excessive and irrational. True there would be some differential expansion due to the temperature gradients away from the source of the fire, but it seemed absurd for the thing to be hopping around like a cat on hot bricks. He scolded it: "Oh don't take on so – a transformer you are, that's all – a core of iron, some copper windings and cooling pipes. All this fuss! What do you think you are, eh? A nuclear pile having a meltdown? China syndrome? Pah!" He laughed at the absurdity of this conversation. But it seemed to him that the transformer replied: it fizzed suddenly into life, animated as Frankenstein's monster by a miniature flash of lightning that arced suddenly across the structure and extinguished itself with a loud bang. Simultaneously, a block of streetlights in the distance disappeared into darkness. He chuckled to himself. This was like a magic show. He admonished the transformer with a wagging finger: "That'll teach you." The transformer groaned and creaked and finally let rip with another minor explosion, rupturing one of the main coils and spewing out boiling oil which ignited in a spectacular ball of orange flame. It seemed to Steiner as if it had built up a lethal fart within its coils. He laughed aloud at this thought. A siren wailed in the distance.

He stared grimly at the letter and the banknote. He would defy her; he would burn them both. It was after all an absurdly small amount of money – ten marks – ridiculous as a present, ridiculous even as a ruse. He was reminded of the similarly small amount of money that she had contributed to the bills after she had left. But her calculation was correct: he could not bring himself to throw even that small note on the fire. Perhaps that was it! Its very lack of value gave it the pathos of her other cheap possessions that had been so precious to her. He sealed the envelope and wrote, 'Gone away'. across the address.

The police arrived in convoy with flashing lights and wailing sirens, along with a fire engine and a truck from the power station. The fire crew went to work. The policemen approached Steiner. They were three – two young, officious, angry-looking, and one older and senior. He peered at Steiner curiously.
"Professor Steiner, isn't it?"
Steiner nodded. He recognised the man as the local police captain.
"What happened, sir?"
One of the younger officers flared up angrily: "Sabotage – that's what it is."

Steiner agreed vaguely: "Yes – yes – that's it exactly – an act of sabotage."

The captain frowned. "Did you see anything, professor?"

Steiner was humbled by the man's deference; it seemed a poor trick to play on him. "I set fire to the transformer. It is, as your young chap so correctly observed, an act of sabotage."

"You did this?" The captain's eyes narrowed shrewdly. "Come now, professor. This is a serious matter – not some student prank that can be covered up. The penalty for this…"

"I gathered up some dried grass and broke up some of the fence, and I lit it with a match. I have them here in my pocket."

A cloud of hissing steam interrupted them as a fire hose was turned onto the transformer. The captain led Steiner away by the arm. His face was grave.

"I must take you at your word, professor. It is my duty, you understand. But why did you do this – a man in your position – what were you thinking of?"

Steiner knew the words to guarantee his incarceration, although he could not remember just for the moment, why this was so important.

"It is a protest against the system of government of the Democratic Republic – against the state, you understand?"

The captain shook his head uneasily. "Intellectuals!" His grip tightened on Steiner's arm.

The telephone call came the next day. Steiner listened to the message on the answer-machine. Her voice contrived to sound careless.

"Hello – it's Sabine. Hope everything is going well for you. I expect you're surprised to hear from me; my scatty friend Monika has done a stupid thing and sent me a letter to your address by mistake – typical Monika – how long ago since I moved out? I need to pick it up because apparently she's sent me some cash, which I could do with – as ever. Please give me a call. My number is, five, four, seven, three. Talk to you soon."

He replayed the message and wrote down the number before it disappeared by some mysterious process. He fought against the desire to ring her; she had gone to this absurd extreme, and by doing so had humbled herself. Surely his pride was satisfied? But the curt angry reply snapped back at him from within: "No. She made a fool of you once – never again." And this cold insistent voice would not relent, its message of fear even stronger than the longing of his heart to see her. He paced the room, poured a drink, and replayed the message over and over again. The drink softened his pride; he should at least hear what she had to say – if he denied her that, he would be denying himself, and would be tormented for the rest of his life with the doubt of what might have been. The cold voice snapped back at him: "If she has something to say, let her say it – no more games." He poured another drink and continued his pacing. The inner voices argued around in circles. Eventually his thoughts took another turn, wondering what had driven her to such extremes to make contact with him.

He froze suddenly in his movement and broke into a sweat at a new thought – at the shame of it, and the nearness of his escape. It was the same guess that he had been so scornful of before, but with a terrible twist to it: she was engaged to be married, but at the last moment, true to her nature, she was panicking. She needed desperately to see him to dispel the ghost of their love that still haunted her. Or, even worse, perhaps she remembered him now only as a friend and would turn to him as a confidante, just as she had to Boris in the past, careless beyond belief of his feelings.

He drank again, but this time the vodka succoured only the belligerent voice of his pride. He tore up the scrap of paper with her telephone number on it and scattered the pieces on the fire. Let her rot in hell!

His journey in the police car was a confusion of light and noise that muddled and irritated him. At the police station he was annoyed to find himself ignored. People of all sorts passed – smoking, drinking and even eating while they walked about, as if they had got up late and were breakfasting on their feet. They either ignored him or stared insolently at him. Fatigue muddled his thoughts so that he struggled to remember why he was in this place. He knew it was something bad, and that he wanted now to go home. If he got up, perhaps someone would help him on his way. But now the room was empty and the door wouldn't open; he struggled with it but the mechanism was unfamiliar and ridiculously complicated. He called out but no one came. He pulled at the door in anger, annoyed at the absurdity of a door that was so badly designed. At last it gave way; he must have found the secret of the mechanism. Something pulled at his arm. He was amazed and delighted to find Hirsch tugging playfully at his sleeve. He shared the joke.

"Hirsch – pulling at my arm – it's not like you to be so childish, old friend."

Another face appeared. Steiner shrank back in fear. It was the man from the Interhotel, the man who had followed him on holiday. He was talking to Hirsch in a familiar way. They must know each other. This was an unpleasant discovery. He turned to Hirsch.

"Be careful of that man; he's dangerous – how do you know him?"

Hirsch looked surprised. "His name is Gregor; he's the doctor in charge. I've not met him before – but you say you have?"

Steiner opened his mouth to reply but thought better of it. This was a strange situation. He was not sure he believed Hirsch; he didn't seem his normal self; he appeared to have an intense and suspicious look about him, as if Steiner had surprised him in the middle of some not entirely honest pursuit. He must think carefully about this.

Hirsch's expression returned to normal. "I'm to take you home to pick up some clothes – can't leave you there though – sorry – doctor's orders. I've got to take you to hospital afterwards."

Steiner smiled with relief; this was the old friend he

knew and loved. "That's all right. I won't make a fuss. Something's not right I suppose."

Hirsch pursed his lips with the characteristic ill humour that those who knew him well would recognise as concern. "Don't know yet." His mouth worked with some emotion. "I'll not tell you any lies, if that's what you want."

"I'd like that, Hirsch. Thank you."

Hirsch turned suddenly away.

In the days after receiving the letter, his heart leapt at every ring of the telephone and at every letter through the door, but she made no further contact. He was surprised, remembering the almost comical speed with which she had turned up at his door after contacting him before. He imagined her pacing some strange room in agitation, waiting for his call that didn't come; he imagined that his silence would provoke her to confront him, and in his heart he awaited this eagerly. He felt a complacent satisfaction at the thought of the inevitable contact to follow that he had ensured by his inaction. But weeks turned to months and he heard nothing from her.

He packed a case with clothes and toiletries to humour Hirsch who stood over him: "Face flannel – you'll need that – maybe take two, just in case."

And Steiner indulged his friend: "Whatever you say – three if you think it better."

And when the case was packed, Hirsch busied himself putting the apartment to order, reattaching curtains and righting furniture.

Steiner followed his friend around, protesting: "Now leave that. I can do that later. Its not every day you come to visit me. We should sit and talk. I don't invite guests in to do my cleaning. Sit down and let me pour you a drink."

"What's happened here? It looks as though the place has been ransacked."

Steiner's impatience grew to anger. "Now come on – enough of this. All this fuss about a bit of untidiness – its not like you, Hirsch – we're scientists – since when have we cared about such trivia when there are real things to talk about?"

Hirsch relented: "Come on then. I'll get the drinks – we'll sit for a bit and talk – then we must go."

He had persuaded himself that what appeared now to be the final break in communication with her was for the best, that, although painful at first, it would eventually bring peace of mind and forgetfulness. But the reality was different. The vacuum that his life had become was filled with ever more poignant memories, which were replenished by strange dreams. The settings of these dreams never varied. He sat with her, together and apart, in darkness, just as they had on that last night before he left – and, just as then, the knowledge was with him that all was over between them. But they continued in each other's company night after night, engaging in endless conversation that was both a blessed relief to find her still there with him, and a torment to know that it was over between them. Even in the misery of these dreams, he was supported by a constant hope that, as the dialogue between them continued, she could turn to him again – and it was a sickening disappointment to be awoken in the morning by the first sunlight – her ghost in flight before it.

He came to regret that lost opportunity to answer her letter; he resented the perversity of his nature that had denied it and, in rebellion against it, he determined that he would now actively seek an encounter with her. He dressed in his best clothes, fortified himself with vodka and, with a terrible trepidation mixed with the romance of anticipation, took to frequenting the one place where he might find her: the dance-hall.

His first foray was on an evening in the middle of the week, when she was unlikely to be there; he wanted to refamiliarise himself with the place after so long an absence. Nethertheless he was so weakened by the possibility of her presence that he had to divert twice for vodka before finally summoning the courage to push open the doors and stagger over the threshold. The place was unchanged, and still mystically infused with her presence as if she had left moments before, her perfume lingering in the air.

This was the first of many nights. She was never there, but the place became a shrine to him. His visits became a precious ritual, although he became increasingly certain that she no longer came there. And then, one night, she was there.

He had little knowledge of his journey, aware only that he was on a trip out with his very good friend, Hirsch. His consciousness subsided to a murmuring conversation in which Hirsch's real replies merged with the imaginary, only at the moment of parting snapping into a stark dissonance as Hirsch bade him farewell.

"Bye, old chap. I'll leave you now. You're in good hands and I'll be back soon. Schellenberg's coming this afternoon so you won't be on your own for long."

He stared after Hirsch's retreating figure and moved to follow, but a tug on his arm restrained him. A short dumpy woman with a huge bosom chuckled at him as if he had made some joke. "Come on now, professor – this way." He allowed himself to be led along what appeared to be a corridor, but as they moved further in, he saw that the sides were curved like a tube, and that they were descending steeply. Finally they stopped before a magnificent spiral staircase of glittering crystal that led deep into the earth.

His examination of the faces in the dance hall was cursory that night; he had long lost the expectation of her being there. Being a weekend, the place was busy; the dance floor began to fill as the pace and the volume of the music was turned up.

He happened to glance across the floor. She stood still amongst the dancers; her face was turned in concentration towards him. He froze. They stared at each other. Dancers moved around her, the central figure in a dramatic opera.

She stooped slightly forward in a strangely submissive posture. She moved slowly towards him. Her face was deathly pale and her expression frozen – as if some terrible event had occurred in her life from which she had not recovered. It was only when she drew close that he saw the hint of a smile about her lips and mouth, a smile that was artless shy and caressing, a smile that told of her pleasure and joy at seeing him.

And he couldn't bear it. He turned suddenly, frantic to get out; he reached the door without looking back, and sprinted away. He slowed only when out of breath. A surge of hysterical laughter burst out of him, that could just as easily have come as tears. This then was the truth; the answer to a question that had lain in wait for him for so long: he could not bear the pain of her; he could never see her again.

People milled around him shouting or muttering to each other and to themselves. Steiner did not know where he was or how he came to be here – only that he had lost his way and that he was underground. He retained a memory of his descent through a tube and the unexpected magnificence of the spiral staircase. He needed to find his way home; then all would be well again. But first he needed to fulfil a more immediate need: to find a toilet. He looked around and suddenly understood that the apparently erratic movement of his roommates was in fact a complex shuffling dance. This made sense; dancing, like so many other innocent past-times, was prohibited here; and the dancers furtively disguised their steps by blending them with apparently aimless movements. He caught sight of the immensely bosomed woman (who he knew now to be a jailer, though not of the worst type) weaving her way through the dance. His first impulse was to hide from her, but the urgent pressure of his bowel was insistent.

"Please, Fraulein – I need the lavatory."

She laughed and took his arm gaily, almost like a lover, and led him through a maze of tubes and stairways. She opened a door for him but stood partly in the way so that he had to press himself past her enormous bosom. She giggled like a schoolgirl and pressed herself provocatively against him. He could smell her sweat; he sighed resignedly; this could not be a dream, not if he could smell her sweat. An absurdly long bank of gleaming white porcelain urinals ran along the length of one wall. But these were no good; he needed a lavatory. He made his way to a row of closed doors and found to his relief that one opened.

The jailer was waiting for him outside. She must have seen him looking at her chest because she had changed into a provocative half-open blouse, and from the way she blushed and giggled, he guessed that this was for his benefit. She led him away; her hand slipped into his and her hips bumped against him.

Years passed. Steiner did not forget her but his memory of her slowly diminished so that even when, at times, it was reawakened, some of the incidents now were indistinct and uncertain.

After ten years, he remembered her only occasionally – with a sharp painful spasm, as some incident triggered a memory from that time.

The block of blue paper – which was a sandglass of Steiner's life – had diminished to half its original thickness, reflecting accurately his arrival at middle age. On a particular day, he noted a number from the pad into his diary and reverently tore the top page away with a sigh that was graduated to the diminishment of the pad.

His sigh turned to an exclamation of surprise as the torn away page revealed the unexpected sight of writing underneath; and the surprise turned to the most profound shock as he recognised the fluid but precise hand. He turned the pages, counting six; together they comprised a letter...

'My dearest Franz. I wonder how long it will take you to uncover this page of your precious pad. It amuses me to see you search for an old envelope to write on rather than waste

a corner of your special pad – and when you are caught without, I see how you fit your message into the tiniest space and frown at this sacrilege – funny sweet Muffelchen. It makes me feel close to you – it is a little peculiarity we share: to treasure our trinkets from childhood that no one else would give a fig for. If I had to answer why I loved you, I think this would be on the list – at least it would count as one of the first things I noticed about you and that drew me to you. And so, dearest, I have made my calculation: at your present reckless rate, one page will last you perhaps a month before you are done with it and throw it so carelessly away (now there we are different! I could not do that; I would keep my precious pages somewhere safe). This of course can only be an estimate in view of the unpredictability of your habit – sometimes not a thing for weeks, and then you'll go mad and fill three pages in one go; such a wild thing is a man! Well then, a page a month it is; and we are now a hundred pages down. I can see a clock spinning just as in one of Schellenberg's mad dissertations on relativity. (Has enough time passed to own up to my belief that the dear professor is truly completely mad? And has enough time passed for you to forgive me for that thought – and of course for squandering all these precious pages?) What will become of us my dearest love? How strange that I can open my heart to you like this, safe in the knowledge of the one hundred months it will take for you to know this. Am I so safe though? Will you not turn to this page with a sigh of regret for its predecessor (as you always do!) and read this, and then storm into the sitting room with these wasted pages in your hand? Is it possible that we are still together, Franz – or is there another now, watching you read these pages – and will she be jealous? Let me give her something to be jealous of – and forgive me for wasting another page but I'm not going to cram this into a corner – I love you, Franz, for now and for ever – Sabine'.

He stared at the pages in amazement. The effect of the note was astonishingly painful; sometimes over the past years he had memories of her that were fond and nostalgic – but *this was different; this was horrible.*

He found himself alone in his apartment. Someone had been messing around with the furniture; nothing was in the right place – and, worse than that, someone had resurfaced his table and placed it in the middle of the room where anyone could trip over it; it should be over by the window where it had always been. He started to pull at it but it was too heavy to lift; he would have to drag it. A familiar face appeared from nowhere and he dropped the table-end in delight.

"Schellenberg! My dear chap – have a seat. I'm sorry the place is such a mess – someone's been fooling around with the furniture. Can I get you a drink?"

Schellenberg smiled awkwardly. "You're in a bit of a muddle I think. It's a shelf – better leave it, don't you think? It's screwed to the wall; you'll only hurt yourself. I'm just having a talk with the doctor; then I'll be with you."

Steiner caught sight of a shadow in the corner of his eye. He rubbed his eyes. His field of vision was irritatingly limited: all in shadows except for the centre: that was bright enough; he could see Schellenberg's suit flashing and shimmering with all sorts of colours. And Schellenberg, uncharacteristically, puffed out his chest and swung himself from side to side at the hips, to give full effect of his dazzling suit. Steiner chuckled out aloud.

"That's a flashy bit of shmutter for you, Schellenberg. If it wasn't for Sylvie keeping you in order, I'd think you were up to something, old friend."

The shadow in the corner of Steiner's eye suddenly gained definition and turned towards him. He stepped backwards in fear; he knew this face – an evil face he had seen before; he could not remember where or when, but, from the familiarity of it, he knew that it was an ancient evil that had been with him since earliest memory. He studied the face warily, and was relieved to find that it was not at this moment malignant or hostile; he must humour it and not give it any opportunity to turn on him. The face smiled, which was a relief to Steiner, although it did strike him as a little absurd that such a long, lean, serious, aesthetic face should smile.

"How are you today, Professor?"

Steiner muttered a politeness. Perhaps he had misjudged the face; it was, after all, with Schellenberg. He sighed with pleasure at the memory of Schellenberg and checked to see that he was still there. They were moving now, going somewhere. A hand extended before him, pointing. "There's a fine view from this window. I'm sure the professor will enjoy it." Steiner followed the pointing finger to a sheet of glass, shimmering with grey electric light that hummed and fizzed like a faulty cathode-ray-tube; it snapped suddenly into focus. It took him a moment to see what was happening: something was on fire. It was a horse! He leapt back with a cry of horror. The horse's eyes were wide with terror; its mane was ablaze. An evil-looking gypsy, stripped to the waist, held the halter in a tight grip; the man's muscles bulged at the effort of holding the poor creature; and, behind, a grey stallion mounted it in a frenzy of lust, oblivious, in its sexual frenzy, to the poor beast's agony. Steiner cried out: "Stop it – for God's sake!" He turned in horror; the face was unmasked – the evil demon he had seen before. Steiner felt his urine flow. The face sneered; and turned away from him. Steiner saw that Schellenberg was turned to that terrible scene with a smile of complacency. Steiner sank to his knees.

"Oh, God, Karl – you – you of all people – oh, God in heaven!"

He was profoundly affected by the discovery of the letter. He was conscious above all of the cruelty of this trick, even though he was aware, too, of a fault in his logic in concluding this: he connected the devastating consequence to her intent; he did not allow any other possibility – she had done this with malice, delighting in the thought of its effect on him in years to come.

The balance of his life was once again thrown into turmoil. He relived every event of their affair, tormenting himself with memories and regrets. He longed above all for any news of her; he knew that she had left the laboratories some years ago, but he had been too proud to make enquiries of her. Indeed, the only person he knew who might have any knowledge of her was Boris. He too was due to leave shortly, and all possibility of contact with Sabine would go with him. This thought decided him; he called on Boris one evening, stifled his pride and asked of news of her.

Boris replied carelessly: "Sabine? I wonder what happened to her – last I heard she was engaged to some bigwig in the party. I think that's why she left; there was some sort of scandal: he was married if I remember rightly – but that was years ago. I've not heard anything since then – disappeared off the face of the earth for all I know..." he directed a sour look at Steiner "or care, for that matter." Steiner managed to appear indifferent until back in his apartment; then he broke down – this was finally the end; he knew he would never see her again.

He studied the character sitting at his side with compassion; poor fellow was not right in the head. There was, he admitted, a comical aspect to this: he had engaged the man in conversation and had imagined that they had held an intelligent conversation – but when Steiner had fallen silent, what he had taken for replies from the man, continued as a monologue.

He looked with pity on his companion. He was tall, stooped and angular, as if once athletic. His speech was apposite to his appearance: intense, earnest and sincere, as if troubled by a matter of morality. Steiner could not make sense of his words; perhaps he was a foreigner, but it was not a language he recognised. And strangely, when the man fell silent, his flow of expressions continued as if the skies had clouded over and the debate had retreated indoors to continue out of sight.

Steiner turned as a movement caught his eye. He was just in time to see a black shadow pass across the wall at his side. All was still but he felt his senses aroused: there was something familiar in the figure he had fleetingly glimpsed – and suddenly his heart raced and he flushed with a heat that seemed to irradiate his body in an instant. Somehow in this subterranean prison, she had found him. That silhouette was unmistakable; he even knew her mood from the snaking movement: wanton, fey, abandoned and laughing. As if in reply to his thoughts, so faint and slow that it could have been in his head, came the chiming tune from her locket – increasing tentatively, as if shy to announce her presence in this place. He got to his feet, straining his ears. His tears fell like rain; she had come to him – and finally he was ready for her, with no care as to his appearance or hers; love like theirs transcended the physical. This separation had been foolish; they both knew it; too much time had been wasted. At last they were to meet. But the chiming tune receded now, and he must follow; he understood and forgave her shyness – to have followed him with such determination – at the last moment it was only right and chivalrous that he should be the one to make that final approach.

She was close-by; the chimes beckoned. He quickened his pace through the tube. An arm pulled at his sleeve. His anger and impatience at this untimely interruption was dissipated by the sight of the ample jailer pulling him towards her. Her blouse was stretched almost to bursting point by the movement. He could not help but smile; the garment was outrageous, it was almost completely transparent and she wore no bra. She returned his smile with a wink, and jiggled her magnificent bosoms provocatively. He giggled; he had never seen such a lascivious display. There was no doubting that this woman had taken a fancy to him.

He allowed himself to be led. She was in a hurry. He was surrounded quite suddenly by noise. A fat complacent voice was in his ear, speaking indistinctly but conversationally. Another voice answered, then another – all unintelligible but softly modulated and condescending – as a mother spoke to her child. Steiner shook his head, both irritated and amused.

This was a meeting of fools, yammering and babbling at each other, their voices rising and falling, speeding and slowing; but unvarying in their tone of tolerant persuasion. He wondered if they knew how absurd they sounded – one soothing monotone taking over from another. The first voice was again at his side. The speaker had risen to his feet. His voice agreed with his figure – which was round. He moved with a peculiar fussing, swaying motion, and yet when he addressed one or other of those assembled, he bent forwards in a peculiar staccato movement, like a hen pecking at seed.

Steiner found that by concentrating he could discern the individual speeches. The fat hen addressed a dreamy-looking man in spectacles.

"It all turns of course on whether it is admissible to consider actions, five generations previous."

A thin man puffed at a cigarette that emitted a peculiar pink smoke. His eyes rolled upwards to follow the progress of the smoke.

"Five generations, you say?" He considered this for a moment, crossing and uncrossing his fingers with the most extraordinary dexterity and speed. "I see; five – yes – that would be unusual."

Another voice replied. Steiner recognised it with a pang of fear. "Four is unusual, five would be almost without precedent – but, in peculiar circumstances, where pertinence can be proved... I believe those are the words."

Steiner studied the speaker's face surreptitiously. To his surprise, the man's expression was genial. He could understand, however, how easily that face could slip into malignancy. The nose was long and crooked, high to the brows with dark brown close-set eyes in its shadow. This was the peculiarity of the face: the expression was concentrated at that junction between eyes nose and brows. But the other surprise to Steiner was the blandness; it seemed impossible to envisage this face as he had seen it before; it lacked authority, it was the face of a servant rather than a master.

The fat hen spoke petulantly: "Pertinence you say? What

can be the pertinence of these actions five generations previous?"

The bosomy jailer crossed in front of Steiner, swaying her ample hips skittishly. She turned suddenly towards him. "Exactly! But then again, these matters have to be gone into." She winked at Steiner, giggled, put her hands on her hips, stuck out her chest and wobbled her bosoms so that they almost burst out of her blouse. This seemed to cause the fat hen some agitation. His mouth opened and closed silently and he jerked forwards and backwards at the waist in a pecking motion even more furious than before. Someone laughed – which appeared to be the signal to commence a complex stylised dance. The man with glasses pirouetted with magnificent agility; up onto his toes, sweeping his hand forward, his mouth open in a silent aria of love towards the bosomy jailer. But although she giggled and blushed, and was evidently flattered, she turned to Steiner with open arms. Her mouth and cleavage parted. Steiner got to his feet, obedient to this sexual demand. His hands reached out towards her.

"Enough!"

The dancers writhed as if in pain at this harsh command, and fell back before a robed and wigged figure. Strong hands gripped at Steiner, restraining him. And he understood the nature of this gathering, and knew the figure before him by the feeling of dread and hatred aroused within him.

The lips moved and a foul distorted voice spoke. "Where is the accuser?"

A tall angular figure arose with arms extended. He began to spin, pulled in his arms, increasing his speed to a blur – and stopped suddenly, his head held back, falling to one side to study Steiner with a pair of evil coal-black eyes perched above two round bloated cheeks – giving the appearance of a monstrous baby. Steiner stepped back in fear. The face was different, but the demonic features bore a hideous resemblance to those of the wigged judge. Steiner tried to back away but his arms were held.

The judge receded without appearing to move, lowering

himself into a carved ebony chair. By some peculiar refraction, Steiner could see the minute detail of the carvings, and was horrified to see a multitude of obscene leering effigies frozen in acts of violence and depravity. The judge's face, in contrast, was an indistinct pallid blur with a red purse for a mouth, from which his speech emanated in a hiss.

"And the defender?"

A red, dissipated and cowardly face emerged from the throng. "May it please your worship, the professor…"

The accuser snapped: "By the nature of his crime, the prisoner is stripped of all academic title."

The defender demurred. "Quite so. It is not of course my intention to diminish in any way the gravity of the prisoner's crime. Such crimes are of course beyond redemption and command the supreme penalty; that is not in contention. There is, however, a point of law…"

The fat hen cackled: "A point of law!" He shuddered with laughter but the judge's face turned slowly towards him as if on a bearing rail, and the fat hen's laughter turned to a cough. "Quite so – a point of law you say."

The defender continued: "The defence respectfully, allowing of course the jurisprudence of the court to over-ride him, as well they might – and I can assure your grace that any appeal would be quite out of the question…" The defender appeared distracted by the thin man's cigarette smoke which had changed from pink to a succession of all colours of the rainbow, blown upwards in expanding rings – one of which, of the deepest violet, floated past the defender's nose. "Well then – this point of law… It is our contention that…" he took a deep breath of courage, "the prisoner's crimes should not be pursued beyond the fourth generation."

The accuser fixed an evil smile on the defender – who shrank visibly from it. The accuser strutted forwards, his face forming a side-view to his evil twin in the background. Their lips moved in synchronisation.

"So – you – say! Well – let us consider what it is you are so anxious to conceal in this tainted bloodline? This name –

Steiner." He spat the name with contempt. "An innocent enough teutonic name you might think – Steiner, Steiner, Steiner, Steiner... That takes us back four generations. It would be a convenient place to stop – all those Steiners... why, they could stretch back to the beginning of time – except that – they – do – not! The fifth Steiner is not a Steiner at all! He is, or was, a Stuyvesant! A bastard – bourbon – Stuyvesant – and I use the word advisedly – bastard that is – for that is exactly what our friend, Steiner is... A bastard of the aristocracy... An oppressor of the commune, then – whose sleeping menace has awakened in the fifth generation to ply his grisly trade of sabotage, heresy, and parasitism – etcetera, etcetera. etcetera – you know the rest."

The defender's face was red with shame. The ample jailer turned to Steiner with a frown of disapproval which did not match the menace of the accuser; it was more of a mother's disappointment at the discovery of her precious son's hoard of stolen sweets. She had acquired a shawl from somewhere that she closed around her breasts. Steiner felt hot with anger at what he felt to be a gross injustice, even though he was not quite certain of what he was accused.

The judge had descended from his chair and stood with his twin; their profiles now facing each other in perfect symmetry. His distorted voice menaced:

"Enough of this. Why examine this accursed heritage to the fifth generation when one is sufficient – what of the father of this wretch? Was he a party member? Did he – as our fathers – fight with an honest soldier's honour as a beacon in that darkness? Or was he, rather, one of those goose-stepping dogs, fawning before their master's moustache, biting and snarling at the flesh and bones of his victims?" His voice dropped, adding to its distortion. "And did the son, innocent of his father's crimes but shamed by them, attempt to live his life in rejection of that corruption?" The distorted voice reverberated around the room: "Corruption, corruption, corruption."

The thin man looked up and blew a puff of yellow

smoke; suddenly snapping at it with an agile hand, squeezing it, killing it, so that it sighed in its death agony and dripped yellow blood in streams down his arm. The judge turned to Steiner; his face was now hooded with a cowl. "What would be a suitable atonement for the son of such a monster – dedication to the party for certain? That would be the very least; the party that could be the sort of father he never had – suffering for him through those dark times. We can at least be certain of that: a young man of sincerity, who hated everything his father had stood for, would be certain to dedicate himself to the party. And so this Steiner, a socially responsible and diligent worker, achieving the higher reaches of science, would be at least a full member of the party, agitating tirelessly for the good of his comrades…"

The ample jailer's frown relented. Her grip on her shawl relaxed; the weight of her bosoms pushed it apart, her magnificent cleavage oscillated up and down in time to the reverberation of 'comrades, comrades, comrades'.

The fat hen pecked in irritation at a small cloud of blue smoke that the thin man had blown in front of him, evidently with the purpose of irritating him further. The judge's cowl now covered his face completely so that only two glittering orbs of glass coated steel could be seen in the shadows.

"Except that – members of this court – he did not!"

The defender arose nervously, wringing his hands in apology. "Perhaps, what with his background – being, as he was, the son of a villain and a criminal with so much blood on his hands – it would be understandable under these circumstances if the party had not accepted his most fervent application."

'He did not' was still reverberating in the air. The thin man paused in the action of blowing out a tube of red smoke, and the echo ceased. Steiner suddenly understood that these games with the coloured smoke were controlling the distortions of sound.

The judge pointed a long thin accusing finger from the sleeve of his habit. "Not so. The party, in a spirit of reconciliation, allowed for the possibility of redemption through good works. The party made approaches to the accused. I shall call a witness to prove it so."

The defender gabbled anxiously: "Your Majesty, the defence does not question... your word is of course more than sufficient... Truly it is unnecessary to..."

All turned at the sight of a figure getting to his feet. Steiner saw that it was Hirsch, who averted his gaze guiltily from his friend. Hirsch muttered indistinctly. The accuser turned to him with a malicious impudent expression. "Come, comrade – what is your shame that you dare not speak aloud?"

Hirsch cleared his throat. "It is as you say – an invitation was extended and denied, several times – I remember it well. I spoke to him about it. 'Steiner', I said – 'you can't go on like this. You accept the benefits of high office bestowed upon you by the party – it would be immoral to take them without accepting the duty that accompanies them'."

Steiner felt the crushing weight of this betrayal. He had been speechless until now, but this last injustice was one too many.

"Hirsch – I would never have believed this of you – you of all people." And in that moment, he saw Hirsch turn to face him, saw the same venom and malice as he had seen in his accusers, and knew the evil jealousy that had lurked for so long in his friend. This final act of betrayal was to deny him his union with Sabine that he knew was imminent.

"I see you for what you are, Hirsch. I am not deceived. You shall not take her from me. I swear to God, I will kill you with my bare hands before I let you have her." He lurched forwards. The hands that had restrained him tried to hold him, but he was mad with rage and leapt towards Hirsch. The hands pulled at him, insinuating themselves around him, dragging him down. The crowd thronged menacingly around him, muttering threats he could not understand. The light became brighter and clearer. The faces and figures around him suddenly changed position; they were sympathetic and anxious. The ample jailer was no longer quite so ample, her blouse not so translucent. He was not afraid any more – not with Hirsch's sincere and anxious face standing out from the others. Steiner clasped his hand.

"Hirsch – my dear friend – what a wonderful surprise. Forgive me please, I'm not quite myself today. Let me get you a drink, old fellow." He turned away in embarrassment at the tears that welled in his eyes and poured down his cheeks. He felt the grip of Hirsch's hand in his.

Steiner lived in that underground place for another two years, sometimes oppressed by his imprisonment, sometimes terrified by the demonic evil that lurked ever present in the faces around him, sometimes amused by the grotesque comedy of his fellow prisoners – singing in an exaggerated operatic style, dancing their secret catatonic steps; sometimes aroused by the blatant advances of the shameless jailer, sometimes irritated by his surroundings that were prone to change shape colour and sound, sometimes horrified by some unexpected happening: walking into a room and finding the walls crawling with maggots or spiders.

But these episodes were punctuated by evidence of her presence: the chimes of her locket, sometimes so far away that he wondered if he imagined them, and sometimes so close that he held his breath in anticipation of her appearance.

Until that time came that was different: all around him was silent; he lay in his bedroom. Just before that familiar chiming tune, he heard – as never before – the snap of the locket opening; he imagined her long shapely fingers working deftly but impatiently at the clasp. The tune intensified. He heard the pulse of what at first he thought was the beat of his heart, but, as it strengthened, knew were the steady steps of her approach.

The chimes halted outside his room. They were different: somehow more determined and purposeful than ever before. He knew by some instinct that this time they would not fade or turn away. He was afraid, but not as he had been before; this was not the trepidation of the past – he was afraid of her. He sat up in bed. The steps missed a beat. The tune was in his ears, swelling to an appalling crescendo. She was there, paused outside the door – she had only to take a single step and he would see the shape of her – tall but stooped in concentration over the silver locket.

He heard the step, looked up to see her staring directly into his eyes. He did not know by which sense he knew her. He called out, hearing his cracked and breathless voice.

"Maria!"

She drew herself to her full height. She was as she had been described to him: proud, stern and beautiful.

"I've come to take you to her, Franz." She held out her hand. His body froze, refusing to obey her command. Only his hand, trembling helplessly, reached towards her. There was a cruel mockery in her smile. He felt the wetness of his tears on his cheeks for the last time